Vendetta Castle

Susan Marino

AVON
PUBLISHERS OF
DISCUS • CAMELOT • BARD

This is the first publication of
VENDETTA CASTLE in any form.

AVON BOOKS
A division of
The Hearst Corporation
959 Eighth Avenue
New York, New York 10019

Copyright © 1971 by Julie M. Ellis.
Published by arrangement with the author.

First Avon Printing, February, 1971

AVON TRADEMARK REG. U.S. PAT. OFF. AND
FOREIGN COUNTRIES, REGISTERED TRADEMARK—
MARCA REGISTRADA, HECHO EN CHICAGO, U.S.A.

Printed in the U.S.A.

For Karen and Janice Paul

CHAPTER 1

I stood at one of the red corduroy draped dorm windows and gazed somberly at the unexpectedly winter-gray June afternoon, while Suzy—my roommate—concentrated on a last-minute nail polish job.

"It's so raw." Frowning with distaste, I reached to drape my beige suede jacket about my shoulders. No heat this time of year, with the dorm near-deserted.

"Chilly," Suzy reproved. But I knew she was attuned to my mood. After three years at Conrad Hall together, we were close.

What had seemed a fabulous summer job only last night was, this afternoon, filling me with inchoate unease. Everything happened so fast! Wow, it was only four days ago that Dean Benedict approached me—when I was already set to work at the day camp in town for the summer—with this chance to spend nine weeks at Castle Mazzini.

That was how Dean Benedict phrased it, "How would you like to spend nine weeks at Castle Mazzini?" I couldn't have been more amazed if he'd suggested I become the first woman astronaut.

"It's actually a vacation," the Dean had elaborated smugly. "All you'll have to do is spend three or four hours daily reading to elderly Mrs. Mazzini. She's pushing eighty-five and waiting out a cataract operation. The big thing in her life each day is reading the local newspapers flown in from Sicily. You read to her—and the rest of the day is yours."

Ever since I arrived at Harris College, I'd heard the

fanciful stories about Castle Mazzini. How it had been dismantled in Sicily, then reconstructed on the side of a mountain in the nearby Adirondacks. Reputedly, no stranger ever set foot inside the formidable castle, which was supposed to have been a multimillion dollar gift from Carlo Mazzini to his mother, some ten years ago. And here I was, about to spend nine weeks there!

"Andrea—" Suzy's voice sounded faintly troubled.

"Yes?" I turned to her with a forced smile.

"Are you sure you want to go all the way up there for the whole summer? I know it's supposed to be the showplace of this part of the country and all that jazz—but you're going to be so isolated." Suzy pantomimed repugnance.

"Suzy, now you ask questions?" I tried to sound flip. "It's not so far, actually."

"It's miles from even a village," Suzy reminded unhappily.

"Suzy, the Adirondacks are breathtaking." I *needed* a job with the fabulous salary they were paying me, in this era of galloping inflation. I had just enough money from Dad's estate, allowing for no emergencies, to see me through my senior year here at Harris. The summer money would provide a financial cushion for the interval between graduation next June and my settling into a job. This way, I wouldn't be forced to grab at the first offer. "Oh, come on," I jibed. "Don't be so tragic. I expect to have a ball."

"You're going to be sitting up there with Mama Mazzini and a flock of servants," Suzy gloomily predicted, "and you'll be climbing the walls." Suzy was jetting to Europe for a seven-week tour, as a pre-graduation gift from her parents. "You could stay in the apartment down in New York—it wouldn't cost you a cent." But the prospect of being alone in New York, for one of the much-publicized long, hot summers, turned me off.

"I'll have gorgeous chunks of time for lying in the

sun and reading," I prophesied rashly. "And the salary's unbelievable."

"The Mazzini woman must be a shrew," Suzy guessed, "if they're handing over that kind of loot."

"It's my knowledge of Sicilian they're paying for," I pointed out with an effort at levity. "A bit of good luck on my part. The Dean said they were frantic to find someone who spoke and read Sicilian. He remembered my background. . . ."

"All of a sudden, I'm scared," Suzy admitted. "I don't know why—just this kooky feeling that you're walking into trouble."

"Relax," I ordered. "You're worrying for nothing."

But I, too, was feeling morbid about the nine weeks at Castle Mazzini. I'd been feeling rotten since I woke this morning. Because of the date. Four years ago today, my wonderful father—handsome, brilliant, warm—had been found dead in the desert, west of Las Vegas.

Dad had been driving to Los Angeles, took a wrong turn, became lost. When the car conked out, he tried to walk for help. He'd died of exposure. I shivered, remembering with painful vividness.

Dad and I had been especially close because my mother had been killed in a skiing accident at Zermatt when I was five. Dad, a journalist, had taken me with him on his various assignments. For three years, from the time I was eleven to fourteen, we'd lived in Sicily. First in Palermo, then Messina and Catania.

"At least, they're sending a car for you," Suzy said drily. "You may be bored to distraction but you'll be bored in the lap of luxury." She squinted in thought. "Where does the Mazzini money come from?"

"I'm not sure. Olive oil or spaghetti sauces—something in the food line," I said vaguely. "But I do expect to have fun," I said with determined optimism. "Lots of people go to the Adirondacks for the summer—I'll find some of them. Even if I have to hike to the nearest village." It would have been nice to have a car, I thought wistfully.

"If it doesn't work out, then cut out," Suzy ordered. "They can't stop you."

I was striving to brush aside these last minute misgivings. Actually, I'd allowed the Dean to maneuver me into this situation. It was he who arranged for my release from the day camp, phoned the Mazzinis to say I would be available. He'd told them one white lie, I remembered humorously—he'd said my parents were touring Europe, would be back the last week in August. That was to guarantee me some slight vacation time on my own.

"I think the Dean bulldozed you into the job because he figured he owed the family a favor," Suzy said with an air of defiance. "We know they made a contribution to the building fund."

We heard a car pulling up in the driveway. I stared avidly out the window at the long, black limousine.

"That must be the car." I reached for the valises at my feet. My heart was suddenly thumping.

Suzy slid to her feet.

"I'll help you downstairs. I still wish you were going down to the apartment for the summer."

We hurried down to the foyer with my valises. My trunk would be stored in the dorm. I was feeling nostalgic about the summer break. Suzy was the closest thing to family I had. I had distant cousins in Texas and Florida, none of whom I'd seen since I was five. Nobody—except for Suzy and the Dean—knew that I was going to Castle Mazzini for the summer.

The black Cadillac pulled to a smooth stop. A short, swarthy man in black suit and black tie—what seemed to be a reluctant concession toward a chauffeur's uniform—strode up to the door.

"I am here to drive Miss Grant to Castle Mazzini," he announced, his accent heavily Sicilian. He looked inquiringly at Suzy, who is dark-haired and dark-eyed and voluptuously built.

"I'm Andrea Grant," I said quickly, sensing that my ash blonde hair, my fair skin and blue eyes, would hardly find favor with him.

"I am Aldo," he said stiffly. He nodded toward my luggage. "These are yours?"

"Yes."

Why did I feel such a melodramatic foreboding at the sight of the Mazzini chauffeur? Because he seemed so distrustful of me? Probably, he ate too much pasta for lunch, drank too much wine—and now he was feeling the results.

"Andrea, I'll be back in mid-August," Suzy reminded, hugging me affectionately. "I'll buzz you as soon as we get settled."

Why did Aldo stare at Suzy with such hostility? I had a right to receive phone calls! They wouldn't come to the castle collect, I jibed at myself with an effort at humor.

I climbed into the rear of the car, waved goodbye to Suzy, who stood at the door with her normally vivacious face grim with concern. But Suzy had this up and down temperament, I coddled my own unease. Suzy was always switching from highs to lows.

I didn't want to acknowledge that Suzy had been against my taking this job from the beginning. Up till this morning, before I glanced at the calendar and remembered the anniversary, I'd been caught up in the adventurous aspect of the summer. I'd adored living in Sicily. I recalled the gaiety, the warmth of the Sicilians, the air of make-believe that made the country so delightful. Why should I suddenly be fearful?

Don't think about the weeks ahead. *Think about now*. What a luxurious car! Television, bar, telephone —a custom Cadillac, naturally. Air-conditioning—but that wasn't needed today.

Aldo sat tense and taciturn at the wheel, yet with an air of pride as though being the Mazzini chauffeur carried a special distinction. I tried to relax against the luxurious white leather upholstery. I was too tense, too uptight with the newness of the summer stretching ahead of me.

We skirted the familiar business section of town, cut off toward the highway, bearing north toward the Adirondacks. The mountains rose majestically in the distance, today clothed in clouds.

I knew the castle was only thirty-five miles from the campus. At the speed we were traveling we should be there in thirty minutes. Aldo swung left, swept onto the impressive Northway, the Cadillac never betraying our speed.

I watched the license plates of cars we passed. Quebec, La Belle Province. New York, Georgia, Louisiana. And then I was caught up in the towering beauty of the mountains as we climbed high. Mountains on either side. Mountains rising ahead of us.

I was almost sorry when we swung off the Northway. For a little while I'd been caught up in a state of well-being. Now my heart was thumping because I knew we'd soon be approaching the Castle Mazzini. Was it as fabulous as rumor insisted?

We drove for another ten minutes—still in austere silence—and then, from the way Aldo leaned forward over the wheel, I knew we were approaching our destination.

Aldo made a sharp right, onto a narrow, winding, obviously little-traveled road. Wide fields sprawling on either side. A rundown farm with sagging barn on the left. And then arose a high stone wall that seemed to extend endlessly—and I knew that somewhere behind this wall stood Castle Mazzini.

I leaned forward, avid for my first view of the castle. We slowed down at the approach of high, wrought-iron gates set within the stone wall. Aldo touched the horn lightly, turned in toward the gates.

A man, taller than Aldo, with massive shoulders and powerful hands, emerged from a small cottage set just within the gates, pulled the gates wide so that we could enter. Calling out a greeting as he did so.

My eyes were galvanized in shock. The gesture of pulling wide the gates disclosed a disquieting fact. *The gatekeeper wore a holstered gun.*

Why? Why was the Castle Mazzini guarded by a gunman? No one lived here except the aged Mama Mazzini, as people irreverently called her. Who would want to harm an old lady?

We drove through the gates, along a straight, narrow avenue, also enclosed by walls. All the while, my mind clung to the image of that holstered gun. Why these walls along the avenue to the castle? And then, while I tried to reassure myself that this was part of the restoration, we were moving beyond the walled area into a luxuriantly landscaped courtyard before the castle itself.

I had seen castles like this in Sicily—but that was years ago. I gazed now with awe at the impressive structure that rose before us. Stucco, three floors high, with the exterior, curved double staircase rising to the second floor. A stone balustrade about the roof, which appeared almost flat. The windows long and narrow, with newly painted black shutters. Tiny wrought-iron balconies wrapped about individual windows at second-floor level. Between the double staircase was the entrance to the lower floor, its rooms flanking a courtyard whose brilliant greenery was visible from the car.

Aldo pulled the Cadillac to a stop, hopped out to open the door for me, then headed for the trunk to drag out my valises. Feeling unfamiliarly unreal, I started up one side of the double staircase, admiring the lushness of the flower boxes that lined the terraces, which sprawled to either side of the stairs.

I hesitated before the massive door. I started as it suddenly swung wide. The gatekeeper, of course, had alerted the castle to our arrival.

A short, obese woman in black uniform and white apron stood shyly in the doorway.

"Please come in, Signorina." The accent heavily Sicilian.

I smiled with the friendliness that usually spills forth from me at the slightest provocation.

"Thank you."

The entrance foyer was huge, by American standards. I supposed this was, in reality, one of the smaller Sicilian palaces. Still, I was immensely impressed.

I gazed with candid admiration at the frescoed ceiling depicting the gods and goddesses of Olympus. The walls were decorated with landscapes. The floor, gray marble inlaid with white. A crystal chandelier hung from the frescoed ceiling, and I could envision its dazzling glory when lighted.

"The Signora is waiting for you in the small salon," the maid said, and indicated that I was to follow her.

I trailed behind the waddling, black-uniformed maid, down the wide, marble-floored corridor. Its walls similarly rococo in decor, the floor wearing small patterned rugs—like so many exquisite jewels. Rugs that, I was certain, were centuries old, lovingly preserved.

The woman paused at a double door, opened wide, and gestured with an ingratiating smile for me to enter. I walked into the "small salon"—the size of a meeting-room at the college, without, at first, seeing Mrs. Mazzini. The ornateness of the walls here broken by huge mirrored panels framed in gilt. The wall sconces, lighted against the dreariness of the day, dripping crystal. Here, the floor was made of majolica tiles, set in a geometric pattern. The windows draped heavily in silk. The furniture massive, in harmony with the architecture.

"Signora," the maid said softly, with rich affection in her voice. "Signora, she is here."

Only then did I see the woman in the wheelchair, semi-concealed by the concert grand in a far corner of the room. She was wheeling herself into view now. A small, heavy woman, somberly dressed in black. The probing brown eyes set in a round, dark face, dramatized by the whiteness of her hair, drawn back in madonna severity. The features faintly heavy, face lined by time. A proud old lady, who had seen much,

I guessed with sudden compassion. Who had suffered much, despite her wealth.

"Why you come here, Miss Grant?" she demanded. "Why you waste your time with an old lady like me?" Her tone was affectionately reproachful, yet I immediately sensed alarm in her, despite the innocuous conversation.

"Because I love Sicily," I said quietly, guessing this would please her. "I spent one of the nicest periods of my life there."

A look of pain passed over her face. Adding years.

"Yes, Carlo tells me you know my country. Forty years ago, I made a trip home. Not since." She sighed heavily, then made a pronounced effort to discard her inner somberness. "Skinny!" she clucked. "Skin and bones." But she smiled with a show of good humor. "Still, beautiful—like the northern Italians. Never mind, though, Lucia will fatten you up. You will see!"

But her hands trembled—and this was not infirmity. For an unwary instant, the mask fell away from her face, and I saw terror. *For me.* Mama Mazzini was distraught because I was here. Within the walls of Castle Mazzini. A chill wrapped itself about me. My heart pounded. *Why did Mama Mazzini look like that?*

CHAPTER 2

"Sophia," Mama Mazzini called out in that unexpectedly deep, firm voice which belied her age. "Sophia."

The short, obese maid with the ingratiating smile, who had admitted me, came scurrying into the room with comic opera haste.

"Si, Signora." Sophia shot a sidewise glance of approval at me.

"Bring us some sweets and coffee," Mama ordered, speaking the Sicilian dialect of the South. "And do not waste time gossiping about how pretty she is." Her eyes twinkled when she turned to me. "Carlo wishes us to speak English at the castle, but when he is not here . . ." She shrugged expressively. Pride in her expression, blending with an indulgence toward male weaknesses. "Carlo is my oldest . . ." The eyes were suddenly brooding. "The next two sons I lose. Here in America. One born here, one in Sicily." She gestured a resigned futility, then seemed to discard this mood. "Where you live in my country?" she probed. "On the shore, where the tourists come in such mobs in summer?"

"When *we* lived in Sicily," I said quietly, "everyone ran from the shore in the summer. It was so hot, so terribly dusty." I pantomimed distaste. This handsome old lady, I realized, was testing me. She didn't believe I'd lived in her country. "I remember my father talking about the *sirocco*, which he used to call the hot breath of Africa. In the summer my mother and father would take me to the highlands." I pointedly

16

mentioned my mother because I remembered Dean Benedict's little white lie about my parents.

"I forget about summers. It has been so long." She smiled with ironic apology. But she hadn't forgotten. "My husband and I—with Carlo, who was three, and Nicky, who still fed at my breast—we left our home, near Catania. In 1909, it was, just a few months after the terrible earthquake which destroyed Messina. We had felt little in the South, but I was afraid. So many times these earthquakes. Three sisters and their families I lost in Messina." Her face was heavy with remembered grief. "I was afraid. So my husband bring me to this country."

Mama Mazzini glanced up, an imperious air clothing her suddenly.

"Sophia, here," she ordered. "No, no," she said impatiently, when Sophia set down the tray and prepared to pour. "I will serve us." I realized this was a gesture to show her approval of me.

The silver tray bore a pair of beautifully fragile, white bone china cups, saucers, and cake plates. A hand-painted platter was piled high with freshly baked *torte di mandorla, zuccarini, spinchi* still hot from the deep fryer, lavishly sprinkled with sugar. And *farfallette,* which as a child I had been allowed on special occasions only, because the ingredients included an ounce of whiskey.

"*Farfallette,*" I said with whimsical nostalgia as I helped myself to one golden knot. "Dad used to say—'eat but don't get drunk.' "

"When Lucia makes *farfallette,* hmmm!" Mama closed her eyes in a gesture of ecstasy. "You get drunk with pleasure."

We sat and gorged on Lucia's marvelous cake, reminiscing about Sicily, both of us caught up in memory. Yet all the while, deep within my subconscious, I couldn't shake off the conviction that Mama Mazzini—beneath her animated façade—was frightened. And I was involved in that fright.

"You will wish to get settled in your rooms," Mama

said, when the conversation mellowed into comfortable silence for a moment. "Dinner is early. Because I am an old woman." She smiled wryly. "In the
old days we never sat down to the table before nine.
But now, with age, I am content with the dinner hour
of the children. Six, Andrea. Sophia or Giuseppe will
call you if you are not downstairs."

"Would you like me to read for a while now?" I
asked on impulse, with an eagerness to please. I'd
noticed the neatly folded newspapers, several days
supply, which sat on a small inlaid table by one of the
tall, narrow windows. I knew that for close to two
weeks now Mama Mazzini had not been permitted to
use her failing eyesight.

Mama leaned forward to pat my hand.

"You are a good girl, Andrea." She nodded, a
pleased smile on her face. "The servants read only a
little," she said with resignation, yet with compassion
for this shortcoming. "Not good enough to satisfy. The
young ones—my grandsons and great-grandsons and
the nephews—they cannot even read their own language." Her eyes flashed with contempt, briefly. "Read
to me, Andrea." She pointed with one heavily veined
hand, with a wide, old-fashioned wedding band on
the ring finger.

I sat at the edge of my brocade-upholstered chair
and read at her direction. First, the social reporting of
the small town—much larger now—where she had
been born and had married and had given birth to
her first two sons. Next, the births and deaths. Her
eyes glowed. Her head nodded slightly at intervals,
emphasizing a remembered name. She was back
there, in the small town forty miles south of Catania.
She was part of that existence, for this while that I
read to her. And it was good. . . .

We moved about the rest of the newspaper at her
direction. Then she was leaning forward to stop me.

"Enough, Andrea," she said quietly, with satisfaction. "After dinner—if you are not too tired, you will

read to me again. But only," she admonished sternly, "if you are not too tired."

Sophia was summoned again, to escort me upstairs to my rooms. I felt a pleasurable warmth toward Mama Mazzini, a kind of kinship. Yet that warmth was tinged with a reluctant wariness on my part. It was as though we were waiting—the two of us—for some shadowed disaster to strike.

Sophia led me up a wide, lushly carpeted staircase, the balustrade gleaming from zealous polishing, the flanking wall hung with tapestries, lighted by ornate wall sconces. At the head of the stairs we encountered a tall, slender man with hippie-long white hair and a small white mustache. An astonishingly erect bearing for a man who appeared to be no less than a decade behind Mama Mazzini in age.

"Sophia," he said sharply, frowning. "Lucia needs you in the kitchen." He was covertly inspecting me as he spoke, with a wariness that set my teeth on edge.

"Giuseppe," Sophia bridled, her pride injured, "the Signora say I am to ..."

"I will show the Signorina to her rooms," Giuseppe interrupted with smug majesty. He turned to me, dismissing Sophia with a look. "Aldo has brought up your luggage." Giuseppe was evidently the major-domo of the servants. "This way, please."

It was as though I'd moved back in time, to an Old World culture, I thought self-consciously. The Castle Mazzini must date back at least a hundred years, probably longer. The furnishings appeared decorator-chosen, at fantastic expense. It was almost as though some old Italian family of royal blood still lived within these walls.

I followed Giuseppe down the corridor, waited while he pushed open a heavy, ornate door.

"In here, Signorina."

He ushered me into a sitting room, done in a somewhat lighter style—in deference to its smaller dimensions, I realized with respect. A delicate green and gold dominating. The floor was majolica tiles, partially covered by an exquisite rug that I suspected was an Aubusson. The small sofa, the lounge chair, the chair at the desk, with its delightful pictorial marquetry—all were elegantly upholstered in the green of the window drapes. The fireplace marble-faced, topped by a gilt-framed mirror that extended to the lofty ceiling.

Giuseppe crossed to another door, opened it wide without going inside.

"Your bedroom, Signorina." Giuseppe spoke politely, yet I suspected an impatience in him. Or was it something else? Something less innocuous.

"Oh, how magnificent!"

I stared with undisguised admiration for the room that sprawled spaciously before me. There was a libertine grandeur about the bedroom that touched a vein of drama in me. I could imagine the kind of woman who might have inhabited this room a hundred, two hundred years ago. An unfamiliar breed of excitement closed in about me. I felt myself crossing from one world into another. And I knew—instinctively—that this other world was dangerous.

Suddenly uneasy, I concentrated on externals. The draperies, the bedspread, the upholstery of the occasional chairs repeated the gold of the sitting room, to blend with dramatic shades of plum and red. In an alcove above the bed a massive bronze Madonna, exquisitely executed. A room to live in for a little while—and to remember forever.

"Your luggage, Signorina." Giuseppe pointed, smiling austerely. But he was pleased at my candid appreciation of my rooms. "Do you wish I send someone up to unpack for you?"

"Thank you, no, I can do that," I refused quickly. I retreated from the prospect of one of the Mazzini servants handling my personal effects.

"Si, Signorina." Giuseppe nodded formally, and took off.

I crossed to one of the tall, narrow windows, pushed aside the elegant silken drapes, and saw the small wrought-iron balcony outside. What a superb view! Despite the somberness of the day, I felt exhilarated by the nature painting drawn across the sky. Mountains rising high into the clouds. The clouds brush strokes of grays and dusky blues.

I moved about my room, hanging away dresses, slacks, my cherished pantsuit, a favorite rain-and-shine coat. Stuffing the foldable items into the elegant Mediterranean dresser, jibing humorously at myself because I had no need for the other drawer space so abundantly supplied.

I hesitated, decided to change for dinner. Something about the grandeur of the castle commanded this. I chose a brilliantly printed jersey shift, cut with beautiful simplicity—and flattering to what Mama Mazzini good-humoredly labeled my "skinny" figure. I tried earrings, discarded them, brushed my hair into a pale golden sheen that fell casually to my shoulders, and—feeling myself living in a dream world—left my rooms and headed downstairs again.

Who would be at dinner? Gossip claimed that Mama Mazzini lived here alone, yet with the summer arriving, perhaps some of the family would take advantage of the castle's resort area location. Who would be at the dinner table tonight?

Carlo was her oldest son. He would be the head of the family, I guessed. The Don. Mama Mazzini had talked about her grandsons and great-grandsons, and grand-nephews. It would be a huge family in true Sicilian tradition, I surmised. I felt faintly uneasy at the prospect of sitting down to dinner with these strangers.

In the foyer I hesitated, checked my watch. Mama had said that dinner would be served at six. I was certain it would be punctual. It was now ten to six. I moved slowly down the corridor, drawn by the sound of voices from a room quite far down. Hearing Mama's voice, edged with sharpness.

"Respect, Nino," she was saying sternly. "You do

not become so American you do not respect your
father."

Giuseppe appeared at the other end of the corridor, frowned at the sight of me. As though I were
an intruder, I thought defiantly. I belonged here. For
the next nine weeks.

"Signorina, the family is in the small salon," he said,
seeming to reprove me for roaming about without
some form of prior announcement.

"Thank you." I was determined to play it cool.

I entered the small salon with a fixed smile on my
face, preparing myself for a sea of strange faces.
There was only one. At the sight of me, he rose to his
feet. A tall, brawny man in his early thirties, with a
coarse handsomeness that was beginning to lose out
to increasing weight. Dark hair cropped close, a sen-
suous mouth. His eyes brazen as they swept over me.

"Andrea, this is my grand-nephew, Nino Santini,"
Mama introduced drily. "He is staying at the castle for
a while." I gathered that Nino was not a favorite with
Mama Mazzini.

"Welcome to Castle Mazzini," Nino drawled without taking his eyes from me. His brawny bulk somehow incongruous in the fine tailoring of his silk suit.
"Would you like something to drink, Andrea?"

"Thank you, no," I tried to appear casual.

"A glass of before-dinner sherry," Mama coaxed.
But she was annoyed by Nino's presence.

"I wouldn't dream of spoiling my appetite," I
laughed. "Not after taking Lucia's cakes."

"So skinny," Mama reproved tenderly. "No matter.
Lucia will change that."

"And ruin what is perfect?" Nino reproached,
smirking. "Don't change, Andrea. Don't let them
make you fat and smug." His smile was cynical, reminiscent.

"Go see why dinner is not ready, Nino," Mama
ordered irritably. I suspected this was just to remove
Nino from the room. She was annoyed that he was
here.

"I'm fascinated by the castle," I said, when Nino had left. "When I was a little girl in Sicily, I used to pretend I lived in one very much like this—a few miles from our little house." It had been a fairy tale world, to a little girl of eleven, to visit with Dad friends of his who lived in a real castle.

"When I was a little girl, I lived in a hut," Mama said with remembered rebellion. "I saw this castle, this very one, from the outside. Those were bad years in Sicily. My fathers and brothers worked hard on the land. All the time cheated! Never enough food, enough clothes. Always trouble. And this castle . . ." She lifted her head with pride. "It was occupied by the Baron and his family. The government was bad in those days—the landlords could do anything. They cared only for themselves, in becoming richer. They brought in evil men to manage the *latifundia*." Her face tightened. "So my son—my Carlo—has bought me the castle where the Baron lived. Six years it took Carlo to have the castle taken apart, shipped here in sections, then rebuilt. But he gave his Mama a castle. No mother could ask for more."

Nino sauntered arrogantly back into view. His ostentatious pinkie ring glittering beneath the light of the chandeliers. His tie-clasp centered with a huge diamond that similarly glittered.

"Dinner is ready," he announced, taking his place behind Mama's wheel chair. "Giuseppe says we should come."

Nino propelled the chair into the foyer, with the deference Mama's position exacted, yet I was uncomfortably conscious of the bold stares in my direction. Why was Nino at the castle? I was certain it was hardly his idea of a vacation. I could see him at a flashy resort hotel in the Catskills or South Jersey or Miami. *Why was he here?*

The dining room was, as I expected, a large ornate room, capable of coping with at least thirty diners, rather than three. A multi-crystalled chandelier was suspended from the vaulted, frescoed ceiling, with

the brilliance of its lighting softening the somberness
of the dark, paneled walls. The white marble floor,
too, lessened the heaviness of the room.

"Sit here, beside me, Andrea," Mama Mazzini ordered serenely, when Nino had deposited her at the
head of the table.

Nino sat at Mama's left, immediately helped himself—with something less than Baron-like grace—to a
tumbler of wine. He spilled a few drops on the
gleaming white damask tablecloth. Mama frowned in
annoyance.

"Andrea, a small glass for me, please. The sherry."
Her gaze rested with mild contempt on Nino, who
gulped his wine as though it were water. Mama
Mazzini might have been born a peasant near the
coast of Sicily, but in the vast span of years she'd
acquired something of the aura of a *grande dame*.
Nino's crudeness turned her off.

Mama sipped her sherry with obvious pleasure,
until Giuseppe appeared in the doorway, frowned at
her while he prepared to supervise the serving.

"Giuseppe, one small glass," Mama insisted, her
tone reproachful. "In honor of the Signorina's arrival."

"Is not good for you," Giuseppe retorted stubbornly, but I felt the wealth of affection that flowed from
him to Mama Mazzini. I was sure that he would give
his life for her if this were ever necessary. *Why did
such a thought slide into my mind?* "The Don would
be most unhappy."

"Then we will not tell him," Mama said, almost
gleefully. It was a small game, often played by them,
I guessed. And richly relished by both.

A less obese edition of Sophia was serving, under
Giuseppe's critical scrutiny, two platters of antipasto.
One contained pared honeydew melon, chilled and
served with paper-thin slices of prosciutto. The other—
with obvious appeal to Nino—offered small green pep-
pers, artichoke hearts, pepperoni sausage, celery and
anchovies.

Mama and I shared the melon and prosciutto. My

presence evidently evoked a reminiscent mood, because as we ate the delicately sweet honeydew with alternate bites of prosciutto, she spoke nostalgically about her childhood, bitter about the way her father and brothers labored in the olive and lemon orchards of the Baron. She described eloquently their ill treatment at the hands of the tyrants who managed the Baron's great estate. Nino was too involved in pepperoni sausage to offer comments.

"He eats," Mama said, nodding toward her grandnephew, "like a spayed bitch."

For an instant, Nino was startled. He grinned, shrugged, and resumed eating.

Rosa returned now with steaming plates of *zuppa di lattuga arriciata*—escarole soup. Beamed at my vocal appreciation of Lucia's culinary skills. We concentrated, for a few minutes, on the savory soup. Mama annoyed at Nino's noisy gusto. I suspected part of this was deliberate.

Rosa returned, with a mixed salad, *Bistecca alla Siciliana*—Steak Sicilian, asparagus with lemon and oil, gnocchi. This was Old World cuisine, prepared with artistry. How my father would have appreciated Lucia's gnocchi, I thought nostalgically.

"I ordered dessert myself," Mama said complacently, while the table was cleared.

"Oh, I can't eat another spoonful," I protested.

"You will try this," Mama commanded. "Is not heavy. A bit of fruit. We Sicilians do not like your rich American desserts at the end of a meal. For snacks we eat the pastries and cakes."

"What is it?" I gazed, intrigued at the dish Rosa was placing before me. "Strawberries?" Yet knowing Sicilian cooking, I was certain this was something more complex than a simple dish of beautifully red strawberries.

"Only strawberries," Mama purred smugly. "Sprinkled with champagne and sugar, then chilled. You will like."

Nino leaned back expansively in his chair, enjoying

the small, feminine dialogue between Mama and me. Still, I was discomforted—and I knew she was annoyed—by the intensity of his stares in my direction. But she held her peace until Giuseppe had come into the dining room and personally poured coffee from a silver service for us.

"Nino, tell me," Mama leaned forward with deceptive sweetness. "How is your wife? After four pregnancies, this fifth one should not be causing her trouble." Mama smiled with snide satisfaction as she saw the flush creep darkly up his neck into his face.

"Gina is all right," Nino mumbled, and dug savagely into his strawberries.

Immediately after dinner, Nino—still sullen from Mama's pointed inquiry—took off with a brief goodnight. Minutes later, we heard a car charging down the driveway. Nino, no doubt, going into the village for an evening of carousing at the local ginmill. I'd hardly envisioned him sitting about the castle for the evening, with Mama Mazzini.

"We'll read," I said warmly, when Giuseppe took his place behind the wheelchair. I knew he would have been affronted if I'd offered to wheel Mama Mazzini into the small salon.

"Read a little while," Mama stipulated, smiling gently. Again, that aura of concern about her that evoked unease in me. Despite the smile, she was disturbed.

The three of us went to the small salon. A chill wind was pushing past the draperies, into the room. I'd forgotten how cool it could be in the mountains at night. Giuseppe called out loudly to Rosa, to bring a wrap to Mama. He wheeled the chair to the fireplace, bent awkwardly to coax a fire into being. Birch logs, interspersed with kindling wood, were piled high in the massive grate.

"Bring the newspapers," Mama ordered, pointing to the inlaid table where they lay. "Go back to an older one, Andrea. The others read to me, but so much they miss. . . ." She shrugged indulgently.

I consulted with her about the newspapers, choos-

ing the one she particularly wished because of a
headline that dealt with a member of the old Baron's
family. Giuseppe hovered there on his haunches until
the fire wrapped itself about the birch logs, soared
upward in a blaze of color. Then, while I read to
Mama Mazzini about a jet set escapade of the Baron's
grand-daughter, Giuseppe pattered quietly out of the
room, wearing his air of perpetual distrust. If I hadn't
observed the rich affection between Mama Mazzini
and him, I would have believed that he hated working at the castle.

I read slowly, so that Mama could savor the words.
She nodded pleasurably at intervals. Giuseppe came
back into the room, bringing us cups of freshly
brewed expresso.

"Ten minutes more," he said sternly to Mama
Mazzini, and left us alone again.

In exactly ten minutes Giuseppe returned to
wheel Mama to the small elevator that rose directly
within her own rooms, and was used exclusively by
her. He allowed us a leisurely goodnight, then sternly
wheeled her away to the elevator.

"Sophia is waiting to help you prepare for bed," he
reminded. *"Buona sera,* Signorina."

Feeling alien, disconcertingly alone in the castle, I
walked down the high-ceilinged corridor to the foyer,
ascended the stairs. It was early. I'd settle down to
read for a while, I promised myself. I knew that
falling asleep tonight would be unfamiliarly slow.
Strange bed. Strange house. Disturbing undercurrents
which I found impossible to comprehend. Yet I knew
I was involved in those undercurrents.

I let myself into my elegant green and gold sitting
room, crossed into the bedroom. I'd soak in the tub
for awhile, instead of my routine shower. There was
a sybaritic pleasure in soaking in warm, perfumed
water. No rush tonight. Take my time. Then into bed
with a new mystery, one of the collection of paperbacks I'd chosen for this summer's reading. I would
have been too exhausted to read, I jibed at myself, if

I were working in the day camp. I'd spent other
similar summers, where I collapsed into bed at an
absurdly early hour after cavorting with an ebullient
bunch of pre-teeners from nine to five.

I went to the marvelous Mediterranean dresser,
reached inside for pajamas. Touched the cold jade of
my Chinese jewelry box—a gift from Dad on my
thirteenth birthday. *In the center of the drawer.*

I knew I'd left that jade box tucked in the right
corner of the drawer. I have a hang-up about arrang-
ing drawer space. Dad used to tease me, insist I
ought to study architecture instead of planning to be
a social worker, with my sense of laying out space.
Why was the jewelry box now in the center?

Fighting panic, I pulled open another drawer,
stared at the contents. Neat, small heaps of underthings. But not quite the way I'd set them. I tried
another drawer—sweaters and knitted tops. The yellow knit had not been on the top of the pile!

Hands other than mine had been in these drawers.
No doubt dwelt in my mind. Why should anyone
search my room? Who had been here? *At whose
orders?* Angry color stained my cheeks.

Did someone at the castle suspect me of bringing in
a deadly weapon, with the intent to kill Mama Mazzini? Oh, this was ridiculous! But I stood there, immo-
bile, my heart pounding. Striving for logic. Reaching
out—and finding nothing.

I remembered the alarm I'd seen in Mama Mazzini. I remembered the walled estate, the walled road
to the castle. The air of a guarded fortress that per-
meated the Castle Mazzini. What was the intangible
mystery that closed in about this impressive structure? *What did it mean to me?*

CHAPTER

3

I shoved the drawers of the dresser shut. Fury churning in me now, replacing my initial consternation. I was repelled by the image of those strange hands rummaging among things so intensely mine.

How dare anyone invade the privacy of my rooms! No, I won't be afraid! Why should I be? Go to Mama Mazzini. Tell her what's happened. She'll be indignant. She'll know whom to suspect! She'll make sure it won't happen again.

I strode from my rooms, my eyes blazing. Started down the corridor. Which was Mama Mazzini's door? Now, doubt began to infiltrate me. What proof did I have to offer? Only my word. She was an old lady—should I upset her this way? But *somebody* must be told that my rooms had been searched.

I moved down the corridor with less impetus. Feeling oddly guilty that I was out here, not within my rooms. Why should I feel this way? What kind of melodrama was my mind concocting?

Then I stopped dead. Because I knew which rooms were Mama Mazzini's.

"Nino, I want to talk to you before Sophia returns." Mama's voice was laced with anger. Subconsciously, I realized that Nino's ginmill carousing had been brief. He'd driven away from the castle barely an hour ago. "You are to leave the girl alone—do you understand? Otherwise, the Don will hear about it!"

"What did I do?" Nino was all injured dignity. "I'm being polite to a guest—that's all." Mama uttered a

29

flagrantly disbelieving sound. "This is not Sicily. I
don't need permission to speak to the girl." Defiance
lightly undercoating his words.

"Learn better manners when you talk to me!"
Mama shot back, her temper rising. "I do not know
why you are here at all."

"Because my uncle Carlo wants a man of the family
always in the castle with you," Nino reminded impatiently. "It is the Don's orders."

Quickly—fearful of meeting one of the servants in
this ambiguous situation—I hurried down the corridor to my rooms. Why did Carlo Mazzini insist that
a man of the family always be in the castle with his
mother? More than a gesture of affection. That rode
through with strident clarity, in Nino's voice. Who
would try to rush eighty-five-year-old Mama Mazzini
to the grave?

Did the family suspect me of trying to harm her?
Then why had they brought me here? I shivered,
visualizing those strange hands, rummaging among
my personal belongings. I hadn't checked in my closet. No doubt they'd have been there, too—with the
meticulous care they'd utilized in the dresser drawers.

I'd left behind, in my trunk at the dorm, the collection of mementos from my twenty years of living.
Photographs, movie film from some of those fabulous
trips across Europe and Asia with Dad, letters from
Dad—all intensely personal things that I was glad
now I had not brought along.

Who had searched my rooms? I knew, now, that I
couldn't look anyone in the face at Castle Mazzini—
except for Mama Mazzini herself—without being suspicious. Still, I couldn't bring myself, after the first
flush of my anger, to tell Mama that my rooms had
been searched. I was certain that she would be furious—but not astonished.

I made a point of locking my door when I was
inside my sitting room again. Physically, the Castle
Mazzini might be here in northern New York State,
not far from the Canadian border. Mentally and emo-

tionally, its inhabitants—with the lone exception of myself—might have been living on a mountainside in Sicily.

I abandoned my plans for a leisurely, perfumed soak in the white marble bathtub, settled for a stinging hot shower. Out of the shower, with sleep far away, I stared wistfully at the telephone. My initial impulse on coming back into my rooms had been to phone Suzy. But Suzy by now was aboard the 8 p.m. 747 flight out of International, bound for Paris.

I went through my paperback collection, chose a mystery which had seemed immensely intriguing when I bought it a few days ago, and slid into bed, beneath summer blankets, determined to lose myself in fiction.

I tried to focus on the words before me, to be drawn into the story. But the real-life intrigue here at the castle plagued me stubbornly. It was futile to attempt to read.

I was chilly, even beneath the pair of summer blankets provided against the mountain nights. Close the windows! With a sigh of impatience at myself for not having done this earlier, I tossed back the covers, crossed the room to shut the long, narrow windows against the sharpness of the outdoors. I glanced up at the sky. Clumps of storm-bearing clouds moved about, annexing auxiliary forces like bands of guerrillas preparing to attack. Not even a sliver of a moon in sight. Not a single star.

I shut one window, traveled to the next, encountered some difficulty with the hook on this one. Hearing a snapping sound down below, probably some night animal scurrying across a twig, I glanced down curiously. My eyes fastened on a silhouette. My heart thumping, I leaned forward for a clearer view. Not wanting to jump to conclusions.

No! I wasn't jumping to conclusions. The grounds were night-patrolled. By a man carrying a shotgun under his arm.

I hovered there at the window, my throat dry while

I watched him. There, another snapping branch. He was triggered into alertness, his head movements indicating he was searching the landscape. He focused on something on the ground. A pair of bunnies scampering about in the grass. He relaxed. The barrel of the gun again pointed at the ground.

I knew that it was absurd to attempt to read tonight. I climbed back into bed, switched off the bedside lamp, pulled at the blankets until they were snug about my shoulders. I should be reassured by the presence of the night patrol, I exhorted myself. Instead, I lay sleepless for what seemed hours. Listening for sounds outdoors.

I awoke to the sound of high-pitched, feminine voices down below somewhere, arguing good-humoredly in the dialect of southern Sicily. Sunlight filtered into the bedroom between chinks in the draperies. The sunlight was reassuring.

I threw back the blankets, searched at the side of the bed for scuffs, found them. Without bothering with a robe, I crossed to the windows, to pull the drapes wide. Eager to allow the brilliant morning sun—surprisingly warm—to flood my room.

I glanced at the clock. Wow, I'd slept late! By school standards, late. No matter, I wasn't due to read to Mama Mazzini until ten or ten-thirty—at least an hour distant. One of the servants would let me know when she was ready for me.

I dressed quickly, in Mediterranean blue slacks and a blue-and-green Vera-printed blouse. Surprisingly hungry, I realized, despite the restless night. What a glorious day for breakfast on the terrace, I dreamed. I'd noticed the terrace that extended expansively across the west wing of the castle.

I hurried downstairs, trying to wash out of my mind the misgivings that had taken root yesterday. I was here for nine weeks, with a fabulous salary and light duties. Enjoy this summer. Consider it a vacation.

I headed, faintly self-conscious, for the kitchen wing. Still feeling myself an intruder in the sumptuous trappings of the castle. Last night, Mama Mazzini had said, "Tell Lucia when you're ready for breakfast."

I strolled down the corridor, conscious of the morning sounds. A vacuum cleaner running in one room. Giuseppe ladling out acidulous instructions, behind a half-open door, about the polishing of a specific silver service. A phone rang, off in the west wing of the castle, was quickly answered.

I hesitated at the door to the huge kitchen, with its massive fireplace preserved intact. In this section of the castle, modernity had made easily discernible inroads. Cabinets were antique, handwrought hardware, but were distinctly late twentieth century. The electric range, the bank of wall ovens, the dishwasher, the huge refrigerator and freezer catered to comfort rather than decor.

Lucia, her expansive girth loosely covered by a light, flowered housedress, was peering at the contents of an oven.

"Good morning," I called out effervescently. Some of my earlier trepidations seemed to be in retreat.

Lucia straightened up, from inspecting the contents of her expensively streamlined oven, swung about to inspect me sharply.

"*Buon giorno*, Signorina." Polite but uncommunicative. Most Sicilians are warm and outgoing. But not the Sicilians at Castle Mazzini. "What you like for breakfast?"

"Oh, whatever you usually serve." My smile was rigid. Was Lucia annoyed at having another breakfast to prepare?

"In the breakfast room, Signorina," Lucia said tersely, and pointed off to one side of the kitchen. "*Avanti.*"

"Thank you, Lucia."

I struggled against a flare of anger. Mama would have given her a tongue-lashing if she had seen Lu-

cia's attitude toward me. Head high, I stalked from
the kitchen into the sunlit breakfast room.

Here, an avenue of windows—certainly not dupli-
cated from the original castle—lined one wall. A rectangular walnut table on heavy, wrought-iron legs,
was flanked by black, leather upholstered, wrought-
iron chairs. Walls a dramatic, rough white stucco.
Butter-yellow café curtains lined the window wall.

I sat down, pushed open a segment of café curtains to provide me a view of the outdoors. Close by a
gardener, elderly, white hair trailing down to his shirt
collar, bent his heavy bulk over a sprawling bush
vibrant with red roses. His hands moved slowly about
the thorny greenery with knowledgeable affection.
For him, the roses might have been beautiful, living
creatures.

I was so engrossed in the tableau outdoors that I
started when Sophia, smiling broadly, placed a tall,
steaming mug of coffee before me. Set down a large
pitcher, filled to the top with rich, country cream.

"Buon giorno, Signorina," she said, scrutinizing me
with respectful curiosity. "You sleep good?"

"Oh, yes," I lied. "I always do." At least, Sophia was
a friend.

"Breakfast come soon," she promised. "You drink
caffé." And then she was bustling away.

I sipped the strong coffee, leaving it black, ignoring the cream. In minutes, Sophia was scurrying back
to me again, with her impatient, small steps, to place
with a triumphant smile a platter of shimmering
scrambled eggs and generous slabs of Canadian bacon
and a basket of hot-from-the-oven bread before me.

"American breakfast," Sophia pronounced smugly.
"You like?" Only now did I notice the predominance
of gold inlay in her smile—of which, I suddenly realized, she was inordinately proud.

"It looks marvelous," I approved, and dug a fork
eagerly into the creamy, golden eggs.

"You want more, you call," Sophia exhorted happily.

I ate with serene enjoyment. I, who normally consider juice and coffee an adequate breakfast, was polishing off Lucia's oversized portions of scrambled eggs and Canadian bacon with the enthusiasm of a native Sicilian. With good-humored guilt, I was gorging on thick wedges of still-hot Italian bread, lavishly spread with whipped country butter.

I was just about to indulge myself with a third cup of coffee, warning myself silently that I would *have* to do something about these enormous country breakfasts or I'd leave in August unable to wear any of my clothes, when I glanced up involuntarily, straight into the arrogantly scrutinizing eyes of Nino.

"*Buon giorno,* Andrea."

"Good morning." I was deliberately cool.

He stood there, grinning at me, overly confident of his coarse, beginning-to-fade handsomeness.

"Up so early?" he mocked, pulling out a chair at right angles to me. Why couldn't he have sat at the other end? I could sniff the overly-heavy application of after-shave lotion, the hair-tonic that glistened on the black, closely cropped hair that was oddly incongruous with his appearance. "If I'd known, I would have set my alarm." He leaned back, his shirt open at the throat, showing off his deeply tanned, bull-like neck. "Lucia," he called out. "Hurry. I'm hungry! And bring more coffee for the Signorina."

"No," I rejected quickly. I had no intention of dallying here at the table with Nino Santini, the object of his overbold inspection. Why didn't he go home to his fifth-time pregnant wife? "Thank you, no." I forced myself into a perfunctory graciousness.

Giuseppe appeared in the doorway, with his stiff posture, his watchful eyes.

"Signorina," he said, unsmiling but deferential. "Whenever you are ready, please go to the Signora's rooms. The fourth door down the hall. She will be on the balcony."

"Thank you." I smiled brilliantly, ignoring Nino's scowl. "I'll go right up."

I knocked lightly on the partially open door, at the same time inspecting the splendor of Mama's private sitting room. A massive bank of framed photographs occupied one wall. That would be family.

"Come in, Andrea." Mama Mazzini's unexpectedly deep voice, that so belied her age.

I saw her, seated in a lounge chair rather than the wheelchair, out on the balcony, bathed in sunlight.

"Good morning," I said warmly as I approached her.

"How do you like my garden?" she demanded, gesturing expansively to the rich display of flowers below. Planned, I suspected, to please Mama Mazzini's eyes as she sat here on her balcony.

"Oh, it's beautiful!" I spoke with sincerity, which she recognized. "Grown with love."

"*Si.*" Her smile was rich with satisfaction. "We tried, in the beginning, for oleanders and bougainvillaeas, but this far north . . . She gestured futilely. "But Antonio has what you call the green thumb. He makes wonders appear from the ground."

"Let's see what's happening," I said blithely, reaching for the newspaper on the oversized wicker coffee table before Mama Mazzini. Knowing it must have been delivered only this morning.

"Sit there. Is comfortable." She pointed to the chaise, and leaned back expectantly in her chair. Hands folded with childlike simplicity.

I had been reading, probably, half an hour when we heard a car pull up before the house. With country-oriented curiosity, I leaned forward to stare at the long, black Cadillac. Aldo was sliding from behind the wheel now. It was the same limousine that had brought me up from school.

"Read, Andrea," Mama ordered, her face suddenly taut. "Only Nino's businessmen arriving. No concern us. Read."

I read to Mama for over an hour—skipping from section to section at her restless command. Then she sighed heavily, gestured for me to lay aside the Sicilian newspaper.

"Later, you read more," she said impatiently. "Enough of that for now."

Mama Mazzini appeared preoccupied this morning, yet at the same time possessed of a need to talk. I lay back on the chaise, listening attentively, contributing now and then. Mama talked compulsively about her childhood in the small town south of Catania, about the early days of her marriage, with an urgent need to relive the hardships of that era. In the midst of such great wealth, she treasured the memory of small frugalities she'd learned to practice seventy years ago.

But the morning passed swiftly. I was astonished when Rosa appeared on the balcony to ask about luncheon.

"You eat with me here," Mama ordered playfully. "An old woman can take these liberties." She shot an elfin grin at me, then turned to Rosa. "Tell Lucia the Signorina and I will have lunch here on my balcony. Bring those little tables, Rosa. Oh, and tell Lucia—nothing too heavy."

Mama dispatched me into her bedroom, to bring out the photo album that she kept on the table beside her bed. Enormously thick with added pages, expensively bound in the finest leather. With pride on her handsome face, she showed me the sons, the daughters, their families. But when Mama Mazzini came to the great-grandson, her voice was laced with a special quality.

"My Victor," she said, love pouring forth from her as she pointed to a collection of color snapshots of an unexpectedly fair-haired, brown-eyed young man with features that would have been too beautiful without the stubborn jawline. "Blond, like my Papa," Mama said reverently. "My first great-grandson—and looking at him is like looking at Papa. Only now, all these generations later, Papa appears." She touched a photograph with one heavily veined hand. "Twenty-two, already in law school. His Mama spoils. I spoil."

She smiled enigmatically. "Victor is not like anyone else."

Rosa brought up lunch, using Mama's private elevator. She wheeled the dining cart out, and I laughed, remembering Mama's exhortations, "Tell Lucia—nothing too heavy."

"After breakfast, I swore I wouldn't eat for a week," I laughed.

But the savory aromas that assaulted us as Rosa moved about setting up tray tables destroyed my determination to remember there was a world beyond Castle Mazzini, to which I wanted to return with my normal slimness. Chick pea soup, baked polenta with tomato sauce and cheese, endive salad. A carafe of steaming black coffee.

We both ate with gusto. While we drank Lucia's perfect coffee, we lapsed into companionable silence, engrossed in watching Antonio, working in the gardens below. After a few minutes, I spied Aldo, striding from the sprawling garage to the west of the castle, around to the front. He slid behind the wheel of the Cadillac, and waited. A few minutes later, four heavy-set men in business suits emerged from indoors, in effusive conversation with Nino, who was seeing them to the car.

"I am a little tired after the meal," Mama apologized softly. "Go find Rosa, please—tell her to clear away and help me to bed. I will sleep till four or five. After dinner, you read to me. We must hear what is happening back home." She smiled complacently, yet—still—I was conscious of an impenetrable alarm in her.

I sought out Rosa, delivered the instructions, and hurried upstairs to my own rooms, anxious not to run into Nino. Climbing the stairs, I heard him savagely reviling one of the servants in the kitchen for what was, apparently, a minor infraction. To Nino an infraction.

Nino's ugly vituperations followed me up the stairs. I closed the door to my sitting room, stood there a moment, shivering. His fifth-time pregnant wife should be glad he was away. Nino must be an obnoxious husband. Not a man to cross.

I strived to fit myself into a daily pattern at the castle, wishing, impatiently, that Nino would leave. Mama made a point of keeping me near her when Nino was about, as though not trusting him to keep his promise to leave me alone. A couple of days he disappeared in the black Cadillac for the greater part of the day, returned to be closeted much of the evening in what I gathered was the office wing of the castle, equipped—I'd overheard this bit of information—with its own private telephone switchboard.

When I awoke on my fourth morning at the castle, I promised myself optimistically that, by the end of the week, I would feel completely at home. Maybe by then Nino would be gone. I wouldn't have to endure those hotly amorous glances he shot in my direction at every fragile opportunity.

I went downstairs for breakfast, grateful to miss Nino, hurried upstairs again for the reading session with Mama. This morning, Mama was upset. She was on the phone lengthily with her grandson, Victor's father. Victor had been staying with college friends at the shore, and had broken his foot in a sailing accident.

"At his age, it won't be serious," I encouraged Mama. "They'll have him in a walking cast in no time. He'll be fine."

"How do these things happen?" She gestured her lack of comprehension. "A strong boy like my Vic!"

"You're not to worry," I insisted. "He'll be as good as new in two weeks."

"I hope." She sighed heavily, reached for the just delivered newspapers. "Read, *cara mia.*"

I read, suspecting Mama was missing half of what I reported. She left half her luncheon, was worriedly upbraided by Rosa. I left them to go downstairs for a stroll about the grounds. A pleasure when Nino was away.

I walked slowly, admiring the lushness of the gardens. Flowers on every side that were worthy of prizes at any flower show. I relished the meetings with Antonio, who—unlike the others—was not averse to informal lengthy conversations.

I spied Antonio just ahead of me, working over his favorite rose bush. I headed in his direction. Fine thing, I mocked myself, when I had to seek out the gardener for socializing.

Antonio, I'd learned, lived in the village. He worked at the castle five days a week. Sharply at five each day, he left the castle grounds.

"You should enter those in a flower show," I said blithely, stopping behind him, enjoying the heavy perfume of the huge red roses.

Antonio looked startled.

"Is not allowed, Signorina."

"What about at home? Do you grow these, too?"

"Not like these," Antonio conceded. "These the Don have flown from Sicily. But I grow in the village. In forty years a fine garden grows," he said, his dark eyes glowing.

"You've been living in the village for forty years?" I smiled with warm interest.

"For forty years," Antonio reiterated with satisfaction. "Before that, I run a pizza store in Brooklyn." Distaste aged his face as he contemplated those distant years. "No good! Not for a man like me. I must be close to the earth. In the earth is life."

"You do marvelous things with it," I said softly. "Your family must be very proud."

Antonio's face brightened.

"Even my grandson—Tony—he say nobody grows roses like me. Ah, that's a boy," he boasted, his smile broad. "Like me he will work on the land. He goes now to agricultural college in Alabama. In summer he works on farm up here. But still, he comes to grandfather," Antonio said with pride. " 'Grandpa, what I mix for this plant?' Not too smart to ask questions."

"How many acres are there here, Antonio?" I asked curiously, gazing about at the vast forest that rose on all sides.

"Walled in, eleven acres," Antonio reported. "But the estate covers two hundred acres. Behind is a deer preserve, maybe another four hundred acres. The Don want to be alone." Caution crept into his eyes as they swept about. One did not discuss the Don casually—I understood this.

I walked away from the suddenly busy Antonio. He was upset at having discussed Carlo Mazzini with me. Still the old country Sicilian, I thought compassionately.

This was a glorious day! I walked aimlessly, sniffing the delightful mixture of scents—roses, peonies, honeysuckle, the variety of sweet-smelling shrubs that abounded about the grounds. I was restless, though. Claustrophobia threatening to close in about me.

I hadn't been off the grounds since I arrived. Why not go for a walk about the countryside? Mama Mazzini would nap until dinner. Plenty of time to go exploring. Amazing, how the prospect cheered me.

Could I ask to borrow a car? I knew there were several in the garage. No, I rejected this. Whom would I ask? Mama was asleep. I could hardly see myself asking permission of Nino, even if he were at the castle. The Don, for whom everyone seemed to harbor such respect, was not here. No, a walk would have to do.

I went upstairs, collected a small clutch, pushed a change purse with a few bills inside, and headed downstairs again for my small adventure. I walked from the castle into the sun-drenched outdoors, choosing a path that would take me to the long, walled avenue that led to the public road. How long was this road, I wondered whimsically as I strode between those high, impressive walls? At least six hundred feet long, ten feet high. Constructed at what astronomical cost?

My steps quickened as I approached the gate-house, eager now to be beyond these confining walls, to explore the summer-green countryside. Too far to walk to the village, and I gathered from the servants that there were no buses in the vicinity. Hitchhike? People did that up here, didn't they?

With a sense of anticipation, I approached the tall, wrought-iron gates. With a soaring optimism riding high in me now. This was such beautiful country. If I got lost, I'd simply ask directions. Everyone would know about Castle Mazzini.

"Stop right there!" A harsh, male voice brought me to a shocked halt. I swung to face the massive-shouldered man with the powerful hands, who had admitted us upon my arrival. His eyes nasty as they scrutinized me. "Where you go?"

"Out!" I blazed indignantly.

"You wait!" he ordered roughly. "I call the castle. You wait here."

Trembling with fury, I watched him go to the small cubicle set up just within the gates. To phone up to the castle! How dare he?

I stepped forward defiantly, reached toward the gates—and froze. I couldn't go out. I was a prisoner at the castle. *The gates were locked.*

I swung about, my eyes ablaze, watching the hulk of a man talking somberly into the phone. Then he was stalking out of the cubicle, brushing past me to fit a key into the huge lock.

"The Signora say all right, you go for walk." He grinned, showing off a lamentable lack of dental care. "Signora, she say you not get lost."

The gate swung wide. Head high, I strode past the gates onto the narrow, winding country road. Still shaken that, for a short period, I was a prisoner at the castle.

When I returned, I promised myself resolutely, I would question Mama Mazzini about my being stopped this way at the gates. Time for a showdown! First, my room searched. Now this.

A station wagon whizzed by, a small boy leaning out to wave exuberantly at me. No hitchhiking, I told myself—I was too uptight for that informal kind of verbal communication.

Forget about going into the village. Walk. Enjoy this sensational view. The mountains were fantastic. What country for an artist, with this pastoral beauty all about!

I paused before a single-line fence of barbed wire, behind which a herd of black Angus grazed with august grace. Beyond on a small pond a mother duck was trailed by a parade of young ones. I paused, engrossed—for a few minutes—in their noisy antics. The diversions washing away some of the tension that had imprisoned me.

I pulled myself away from that single-line fence—charged, I knew, to keep the black Angus within the fields. Why did I hesitate about my walk now? Come now, Andrea, I derided myself. Was I going to let an absurd encounter keep me uptight on a glorious day like this?

All right, don't try to hitchhike into the village. Walk about a mile down this road, then swing around and turn back. Suddenly I was conscious of looking ridiculous, walking along a country road with purse in hand. I wasn't likely to find a diner, or a frozen custard stand, along the way!

I walked briskly. On my left open fields. On my right some sagging outbuildings. Further along, I recalled from the drive to the castle, there'd be an old farmhouse.

I struggled to concentrate on the beauty of the scenery, to wash away from my memory the shocking, ugly encounter with the gatekeeper. Yet I knew, even then, that those brief moments were etched on my mind.

I could feel fresh anger rising to the surface in me as I remembered. How did the gatekeeper dare hold me that way? Suppose Mama Mazzini had already been napping? No one at the castle would have awakened her. *I wouldn't have been permitted to leave.* Oh, I would talk to Mama about this later! I had every right to demand an explanation.

I walked along the grassy side of the road, finding the mountain air exhilarating despite my belligerent mood. Strolling around the countryside this way each day would help me keep my cool, as well as work off some of the calories supplied by Lucia's epicurean meals. Would I have to be checked out with Mama Mazzini each day, I asked myself humorously? Or was I officially cleared now?

At what I gauged to be a mile, I turned around and began to retrace my steps. Wouldn't it be kooky if the gatekeeper—armed, my mind insisted on pointing out—refused me re-entry? I'd have to hitch a ride into town and phone up.

I must have miscalculated my distance—or I was out of condition. Before the farmhouse was in sight, I was already exhausted. Puffing from the uphill climb. I wasn't lost, I pushed down a sudden unease. I hadn't turned off the road. This was the way back to the castle. Just longer than I'd anticipated.

With what romantic fantasies I'd approached the Castle Mazzini on my arrival! Now I would see it with fresh eyes. No longer the magnificent, transplanted castle on the side of a mountain. Now, a walled fortress. An armed guard at the gatehouse. The grounds patrolled by a man with a shotgun.

At this moment, I would have been quite happy to have seen the castle just beyond. The back of my legs were aching. My back hurt. Before, I had been walking downhill. Now, it was all upward climb.

I started at the sound of a car behind me. Instinctively, I swung about as I plodded along, to see who was driving up the hill. If it were the station wagon with the small boy, I wouldn't be too proud to thumb a ride the rest of the way.

The car rolled into view. A black Cadillac limousine. Aldo at the wheel. Suddenly—and, ridiculously, feeling guilty—I paused. Nino stuck his head from the rolled-down window.

"Andrea!" he called. "What the devil are you doing on this road?"

"Taking a walk." My voice was edged with defiance, my eyes afire. I stood stolidly in place, waiting for the car to pull up beside me.

Nino flung open the door.

"Get inside," he ordered, scowling.

I was too bushed to argue. I scrambled awkwardly into the car, over his highly polished brown shoes, to settle as far to the other side as I could contrive.

"Thanks for the lift." I was deliberatey flip.

"With all the acreage back at the castle, you have to go walking on this crummy road?"

"I have a spirit of adventure," I drawled, my eyes belligerent when they met his. Still, deep inside, I was scared. I could guess—in sizzling technicolor—the ugliness of Nino Santini. "I like to explore the countryside," I continued with an insouciance I didn't feel.

"Next time, tell my great-aunt to send you out with a car. There are five at the castle," he boasted. He was insidiously moving closer to me. I stiffened in repulsion. He might use the most expensive of masculine scents, but hadn't anyone ever told him not to take a bath in it? "Aldo will drive you."

"I enjoy walking," I shot back. My eyes covertly fastened to his pinkie-bediamonded hand, which was sliding toward my knee.

I stared pointedly into the rear view mirror. Aldo was watching us. Nino noticed. The hand retreated.

"You got to be careful, walking around this area," Nino said silkily. "Snakes in these mountains—bad ones. Copperheads, rattlers. And you hear about animals coming out of the woods. Bear, a couple of times. You don't want to meet one of those characters all by yourself."

His eyes were hotly amorous again, but he maintained his distance, mindful of Aldo's presence. Fearful of Aldo's making a report to Mama Mazzini, I surmised. I was relieved that there was a lock on my door. This creep might just decide to pay me a nocturnal visit, despite Mama Mazzini's exhortations to leave me alone. But the lock was there—would be utilized. Oh, when was he going home?

Where was home? New York, I recalled. Somewhere up in Westchester County. A whole compound of Mazzinis up there, I gathered. Nino had boasted about his jazzy new house, that cost close to half a million. Where his pregnant wife looked after the other four kids, and wondered what woman Nino was chasing behind her back. That was the Old World way, where the wife tended the house and the chil-

dren, and the man swaggered through his private
love affairs.

Aldo honked as we approached the gates. A defi-
nite signal to announce his arrival, I realized. We came
to a halt while the burly gatekeeper who'd tried to
keep me from leaving earlier ran obsequiously to
admit the limousine.

"Rico, you sleeping on the job?" Nino jibed in high
spirits. "Or drinking too much *vino?*"

"No, Nino, no," he declared with dramatic injury. "I
been cleaning my gun, like you say this morning."

We drove through the gates, up the long, walled
avenue. In the car with Nino, riding up this avenue, I
fought off a sudden onslaught of claustrophobia. A
feeling that I might, one day, ride up this avenue to
my death. Oh, I was being melodramatic! Why
should anyone at the castle wish to kill me?

As soon as the sleek, black limousine slid to a stop
before the castle entrance, I jerked open the door on
my side and hurried out. Hearing Nino's laughter behind me. He thought I was running away from a
possible pitch. That was part of it.

My face hot, I rang the bell. The door was always
kept locked. Sophia admitted me with a wide smile.
As we exchanged a few words about the weather, I
saw Nino crossing to the side wing of the castle. The
wing informally considered the office.

Now I climbed the wide, curving staircase to my
rooms, intent on remaining there until dinner. After
dinner, Mama Mazzini and I would go into the small
salon to read, and I'd ask why I was treated as a
virtual prisoner this afternoon. Without her permission, Rico would never have allowed me beyond the
gates.

Mama Mazzini was unusually somber at dinner.
Was it because of the incident at the gates? With
Nino at the table with us, she wouldn't discuss this, of
course.

I tried to appear natural, not to let on how uptight

I actually was. Nino was in jovial spirits. He'd enjoyed the encounter with me on the road, I realized in
astonishment. Why? I was candidly repulsing all his
advances. Or did he consider this a game on my part?
I shivered. I wanted no part of Nino Santini.

As usual, Giuseppe stood at the entrance to the
dining room to supervise the serving. An antipasto
arrived first—sautéed mushrooms, sliced eggs, tuna,
roe, Italian ham, arranged on a bed of crisp lettuce.
Then vermicelli soup, a string bean salad, a gourmet's
chicken tetrazzini.

While I eulogized the chicken tetrazzini, Mama
Mazzini motioned to Giuseppe to come to her side.
Stiffly erect, he hurried to lean beside her. Nino was
all absorbed in his eating.

"You talk to Father Marchesi?" Mama asked Giuseppe quietly.

"Si, Signora," Giuseppe replied, speaking in Sicilian, as though that gave them some privacy from me.
"He will be here tomorrow, as you ask. He remembered, Signora."

Nino gulped down his spiced figs, topped with
fluffs of rum-flavored whipped cream, swigged down
his expresso, and excused himself with gauche humor.
Mama Mazzini was plainly annoyed at this rush act.

"I haven't eaten figs since I was down in Georgia
one summer, when I was a little girl," I said, hoping
to coax her into good humor. "We used to pick them
every morning. And I ate them in Sicily, of course—"

"My Carlo have a friend down in the warm states,"
Mama said, smiled and gestured indulgently. "Carlo
have friends everywhere. But this one, he flies the figs
up for me. He knows how much I like." She leaned
forward with an eager smile. "I tell Giuseppe to bring
you more."

"Oh, no," I protested, laughing.

But Mama was already smugly summoning Giuseppe to her side. I didn't stop her. To Mama, food
was the panacea for many ills. And Lucia would be
pleased.

As I'd anticipated, Mama ordered Giuseppe to wheel her into the small salon after dinner, shipped him up to her rooms to bring down the newspaper we'd left half-finished this morning. I felt a constraint in her while we sat before the fireplace with a fire laid but unlit because tonight was unusually warm, waiting for Giuseppe to return.

Mama talked about Victor. She'd had another phone call from her grandson.

"The doctor say Victor's fracture is a simple one. He expects the foot will heal quickly. I suppose he will go off to Europe again this summer," she went on wistfully. "But before he goes, he will come see me. Always he find time for me," she added with pride.

Giuseppe returned with the newspaper. Mama dismissed him with orders to close the door. I knew she was going to talk to me about being stopped at the gate. She waited for the door to close, leaned forward urgently.

"Andrea, that Rico—I tell him off good when he stop you that way this afternoon!" Her face was vigorously indignant. "*Stupido!* He has orders—know who comes into the castle. My son Carlo . . ." Her face was suddenly deeply sad. "When a man make himself a great fortune, he make himself enemies. We have to be careful—for the family. Four years ago, tomorrow, my son—next to the oldest—he is killed in a car accident. It was—how you say—fixed. Somebody want him dead." She rocked herself in remembered grief. "Four men in the car with him—all die. So we be careful, Andrea. All the time we be careful."

"Please, don't worry about my being stopped," I said quickly, to soften the concern on her face. But in the back of my mind hovered the realization that I hadn't been trying to come into the castle—I'd been attempting to go out. I forced a bright smile now. "I had a lovely hike," I improvised. "It's such magnificent country."

"You know how to hike?" Mama asked eagerly, leaning forward. "You like?"

"I love bike riding," I confirmed with a show of enthusiasm.

"Good," Mama said with relish. "I tell Aldo, bring to the storage room off the kitchen the bicycle Victor rides when he come here. He don't like the big, black cars." She chuckled indulgently. "But the bicycle—you take, ride every day," she coaxed. "Victor will not mind. And that Rico," She glared sternly. "He will not stop."

But if Mama—or Carlo Mazzini, or even Nino—ordered me not to leave, *I would have to remain at the castle*. I knew the strength of the security here. I knew about the gun Rico carried beneath his jacket.

Mama and I settled down to our reading schedule, but tonight Mama was only half-listening. She was caught up in memory—agonizing, in retrospect, over the death of her second-born. I surmised that Father Marchesi, from the village, was coming to hold a memorial service for him. Most likely, a small chapel was tucked away somewhere in the castle.

As though reading my mind, Mama answered this question.

"When I move into the castle, Carlo build a chapel. Is hard, even then, for me to go to mass, to confession. So my son arrange this for me. Tonight, I like to be there for little while. Push me, Andrea," she said quietly—and I knew that this was a kind of seal-of-approval from her, this allowing me to assume Giuseppe's cherished position.

I pushed the wheelchair out into the corridor, then a few feet down, at Mama's direction.

"Through this door here." There was an urgency in Mama's voice.

I reached to pull the door wide, discovered another corridor, leading into the west wing of the castle. The wing which also housed the offices, I recognized.

"All the way down to the end," Mama directed me, because several doors led off the corridor. "The double doors there."

I pushed the chair down the marble-floored cor-

ridor to the ornate, mahogany double doors, hurried
to open them. I gasped in admiration at the beauty of
the small, rectangular room, a replica of the eight-
eenth-century oratories I faintly remembered seeing in
Sicily, in the role of a very young tourist.

"Here is peace," Mama Mazzini said reverently,
while I hastened to take my place behind the wheelchair again.

The chapel was capable of holding, comfortably,
about thirty people; but it was constructed with the
lavishness one would expect in a great cathedral. The
plasterwork that flowed over the walls was exquisite.
Decorative frames, panels of tiny figures depicting
the mysteries of the Rosary, life-sized allegorical
figures set against the wall or in niches. The ceiling
similarly adorned. The floor inlaid with colored marble patterns. Tones of gold and white everywhere,
which lent a lightness to the chapel. The benches
were made of mahogany and inlaid with mother of
pearl.

I moved Mama Mazzini to the position she indicated. She bowed her head, clutched at her rosary
beads. I quietly took myself to the rear bench and sat
down. This was where Mama Mazzini came in time
of trouble. This was her private sanctuary against life.
With the great Mazzini wealth, Mama Mazzini was
an infinitely sad old lady.

I awoke early in the morning, instantly wide
awake. Perhaps, because I'd set a mental alarm. Last
night I'd promised myself I'd spend an hour biking
before breakfast. Deep within, I harbored a childishly
stubborn desire to ride down that long, walled avenue
to the imposing, *locked* gates—and through those
gates onto the public road, without being stopped by
Rico. To prove to myself that I was free to come and
go as I chose.

I dressed quickly, in audaciously red knit slacks
and matching sweater because this early—barely sev-
en-thirty—the morning air was crisply cold. I dug out

white sneakers, a length of black grosgrain to tie my
hair sternly away from my face. Now I headed downstairs. Mama Mazzini had said the bicycle would be
kept in a storage room off the kitchen.

When I strolled into the kitchen, Lucia looked up
at me in astonishment.

"You are up so early, Signorina?"

"I'm going bike riding," I explained, bubbling over
with high spirits this morning. "Aldo was to bring it to
the storage room ..."

"*Sì*, it is there." Lucia nodded vigorously. "But first,
you have *caffé*," she said sternly. For the first time, it
seemed, fully accepting me as a member of the
household. "No leave without *caffé*."

"I'd love it," I agreed enthusiastically. Lucia was
already pouring.

I finished my coffee. Lucia, meanwhile, had
brought the bike from the storage room, placed it
outside the kitchen door, beside her meticulously
cared-for herb garden. I went out to the bike. It was
a beautifully constructed, like-new, English racer—
far more impressive than what Suzy and I shared
back on the campus.

I straddled the seat, rode slowly along the pebbled
path, around to the side of the castle. Swinging into
the driveway and down into the walled avenue that,
inevitably, elicited a sense of claustrophobia in me.

As I approached the gatehouse, I could hear voices
raised in heated conversation.

"Look, I'm Antonio's grandson," a young yet charm-
ingly mellowed voice was saying with strained pa-
tience. "I've told you, my grandfather is laid up with
arthritis. Maybe he won't be able to work for a few
days. He sent me to take his place. I go to agricultural
college—I know about these things."

Tony, Antonio's grandson, I thought with a surge of
interest. My first impulse was to hurry down the path
to help in the identification, but instinct warned me
against this. I, too, was a stranger. Halted only yesterday at this same gate.

"How I know you don't lie to me?" Rico was demanding belligerently. "How I know you don't hit Antonio over the head and come in his place?" To kill Mama Mazzini, or Carlo, or Nino, now in residence?

"The telephone, man!" Annoyance burst through now. "Get on the phone and call my grandfather. Don't take my word—ask the operator for the number."

I was arriving within view now, but Tony was too engrossed in battle to notice, and Rico had his back to me. I stared at Tony, on the outside of the austere wrought-iron gates, and my heart reacted independently of my mind. Thumping absurdly. He was tall, broad-shouldered, slimly built. Antonio had said, "a face like a Botticelli angel . . ." I could visualize the Botticelli angel, perhaps fifteen years ago. Now he was strikingly handsome, despite the hair that hung, dark and shining, almost to his shoulders. Despite the shaggy beard, the faded jeans and wrinkled shirt.

"Antonio has a phone?" Rico's voice was skeptical, his face derisive.

"You don't have to live in a castle to have a telephone these days!" he shot back. "I pay for it."

Tony saw me. He seemed, for an instant, disconcerted. But his eyes, brown and expressive, held mine, and I felt a startling upheaval within myself. Rico swung about with a bellicose scowl, aware of my arrival at the gate. He stared at the bicycle, seemed on the point of some comment.

"I'm going outside," I said coldly to Rico, geared for battle. But part of my subconscious was sending out alarm signals about the new arrival. Never in my life had I been turned on this way! For the gardener's grandson, my mind mocked—at first sight! And immediately, I was ashamed of this initial snob reaction. "Would you please unlock the gate?" I fastened a fixed smile on Rico.

"Si, Signorina," Rico agreed sullenly, reaching for the key and approaching the gate. He stared with hostility at Tony. "Stand aside—the Signorina is coming through."

"Excuse me," I said softly, uneasy about this emotional reaction in me. The chemistry boiling between Tony and me as our eyes met compulsively again.

"Good morning," he drawled. Did he recognize my confusion? Heat stung my cheeks as I considered this.

I have such a habit of making vital decisions on impulse. Dad used to tease me about this. But I knew —unless I watched myself closely—that Antonio's grandson would play an important role in my life. At first sight I knew this.

I biked without seeing the scenery around me. Instead, I saw the handsome, intense face of Antonio's grandson, who was attending agricultural school down in Alabama. Would he be allowed to substitute for his grandfather? Would I see him when I returned to the castle? With the kind of security maintained, I couldn't be sure. But I wanted to see him again!

I rode about three miles down the road, forcing myself occasionally to brake and gaze about. Two men and a woman working in the fields stopped to stare curiously at me. I gathered strangers were rare around here. I waved. They waved back, and returned to their work.

A friendly mongrel with a black patch over one eye came out to greet me from a farm outbuilding, trailed along happily for a while, then decided it was time to return to home territory. I decided it was time for me, too, to return to what was, for these nine weeks, home.

When I was at the gate again, Rico came out— sullenly, without a word—to unlock the gate for me, pull it wide. With a distant smile of thanks, I pedaled past the gate and on up the long, walled avenue.

Self-consciously, I scanned the grounds as I rode along the pebbled path to the rear of the castle to store away the bike. No sign of Tony, I noted with disappointment. But he could be here on these expansive grounds without my seeing him. No doubt in my mind that he'd be able to prove his identity. But would this be sufficient? I wished, with astonishing intensity, that Tony would be working here at Castle Mazzini.

I stowed away the bicycle, my first intent now to make a show of my presence to Lucia and settle down to breakfast. But I stopped, close to the kitchen threshold, tensed in caution.

"Come on, Lucia!" Nino was calling from the breakfast room. "You mean to keep me waiting all morning for that ham and eggs? You getting so old you can't move?"

I cut away from the kitchen, back to the outdoors, to make the long trek all around to the side entrance, via the terrace, where, curiously, no one ever breakfasted. I'd wait a while, till Nino had taken off for the office and that barrage of phone calls he made every morning. Mama Mazzini said it was Nino's task to check with the various offices each morning, no matter where he was.

I inspected my watch. Only eight-thirty. Plenty of time to wait out Nino's tenure of the breakfast room. Mama Mazzini never called for me before ten. I had no intention of providing an opportunity for Nino to make obnoxious advances.

I climbed the staircase to the second floor, more conscious than ever—since running into Antonio's grandson that way—of the unreality of my being here. Sometimes, I expected to shut my eyes and be whisked over to the clamor of the day camp where I'd thoroughly expected to be working this summer. Yet I was here, at Dean Benedict's urging—and here I had every intention of remaining.

Rosa was collecting some small rugs in the corridor, obviously to take outside for beating. I tried some small talk, but she was shy. Or scared. I opened the door to my rooms and went inside. Not seeing, at first, the sheet of paper lying just within the door.

I crossed to the windows, to open them wide to the morning sunlight, swung about and saw the paper.

Curious, I crossed to pick it up. Read the crudely printed block letters. Suddenly, my heart was pounding thunderously. I stared at the words, rereading in a haze of incredulity.

"GO HOME SIGNORINA. GO HOME OR DIE."

CHAPTER 5

I sat on the small, green satin upholstered sofa, and my hand was trembling as I gripped that quite ordinary sheet of white paper with the ominous words roughly blocked out. Who had put this under my door? I'd been away from the castle an hour. It could have been anyone. *Why?* They didn't *mean* it. Did they?

So much happened here behind dark shadows! My rooms being searched, my being detained at the gates—and now, this! What was it Mama Mazzini said that first afternoon? "Why you come here, Miss Grant?" And there had been a deep-seated fear in her voice. Not for herself. *For me.* What had I walked into when I came to Castle Mazzini?

I mustn't lose my cool. Just sit here a while, catch my breath. Wait until Nino is gone from downstairs, then go down and have my breakfast. I don't want to face Nino with this warning. Mama Mazzini. When she calls me this morning, I'll show it to her.

Still shaken, I folded the sheet of paper, slid it into the pocket of my slacks. Impatient, now, to show this note to Mama Mazzini. To share my alarm.

Would she try to send me away? This fresh thought crept insidiously into my mind. I was frightened, yes—but I rebelled at being driven away without knowing why. And there was Tony, whom I'd seen for only a few moments—but who stirred me so strangely. I was *not* going to leave the castle. We would discover who sent this insane note—and I'd stay.

57

I waited restlessly for sounds from below that would indicate Nino had finished his breakfast and moved to the office. With his raucousness which set Mama's teeth on edge it was fairly easy to establish his locale.

"Aldo!" Nino's voice roared below. "Sophia, tell Aldo I want him in the office. *Presto!*"

I moved to the door, opened it slightly, so that I could observe Nino's progress below. There, he was cutting out into the office wing. All right, go downstairs, have breakfast. It astonished me that I could be aware of hunger, with that menacing note stuffed away in the pocket of my slacks.

I walked downstairs, back to the kitchen, peered in with a semi-smile. Lucia was scowling. Annoyed at Nino's high-handed manners, I guessed.

"Go," she ordered with a dramatic sweep of her hands, gesturing toward the breakfast room. "I bring. You want scrambled eggs, sausages?"

"Lucia, anything you prepare is sensational," I soothed and saw her soften under this plotted flattery. "Surprise me."

I left Lucia to go into the white stuccoed breakfast room, sat in a black leather upholstered chair that flanked the bank of windows, and pushed back a segment of the butter-yellow *café* curtains to provide a view of the lush side gardens. My heart suddenly thumped. Tony had got past Rico. I saw him, on his haunches, feeding fertilizer to one of Antonio's prize rose bushes.

Lucia came into the breakfast room, mumbling colorfully under her breath and bearing a carafe of coffee to sustain me until the solid food arrived. I caught the whiff of hot rolls in the oven, and my hunger intensified.

I knew Lucia's mumbling was aimed at the absent Nino. She poured coffee for me, exchanged a wry grin with me—which established a conspiratorial, mutual contempt for Nino—and then hurried back to her kitchen range.

I ate creamy scrambled eggs and golden brown sausages in a momentary euphoria, paying heed only to my hunger and the satisfaction thereof. I paused to listen when I heard a car pull up out front, becoming aware of the aura of excitement this arrival precipitated. Lucia and Rosa were chattering volubly, with an undercurrent of excitement, in the kitchen. Sophia was shrieking for Giuseppe, somewhere on the second floor. She was in the foyer now, at the foot of the staircase.

"Giuseppe! Giuseppe! The Don—he is here! Tell the Signora! *Presto!*"

Nino, too, had heard the pulling up, was shortcutting from the office wing. I heard him greeting his uncle—less raucous in the presence of the Don. Snapping orders at Aldo. Something about the car. Even Tony, absorbed in gardening, paused to listen to the keyed-high sounds of Carlo Mazzini's arrival at the castle.

I could hear the two men, Carlo and Nino, coming into the castle now. They were in the foyer, Carlo talking to Nino about his flight, which had been delayed twenty minutes. Obviously, Carlo Mazzini had impatience with such delays.

"Mama doesn't know?" Carlo was demanding, his voice resonant, commanding. A man of great power—it was there in the voice, I thought with involuntary respect.

Though Carlo Mazzini had come to this country at the age of three, there remained an Old World accent in his voice, the lingering reminder of a child growing up in a household where Sicilian was the first language, and English second. "You didn't tell her I was arriving, Nino?"

"Uncle, only Aldo knows." Nino's voice excessively hurt. "And he only because he must drive to the airport to bring you here. You tell me, keep it a surprise—so I do."

"Carlo!" Mama's voice was joyous as she was

wheeled from the elevator into the corridor. "Oh, my son! My son!"

"Mama . . ." An unexpectedly rich vein of tenderness showed itself. "Mama, you think I'd let you be alone today?"

"You look tired," Mama complained. "Work too hard."

"No, no," Carlo brushed this aside. "I'm fine. Father Marchesi will be here?"

"Within the hour."

How wonderfully sweet, I thought, for a man of Carlo Mazzini's position to make the trip all the way up here, to spend the anniversary of his brother's death with his aged mother.

"We will wait in the chapel for him," Carlo said gently. But the master in his castle.

"First you eat," Mama commanded. "Giuseppe, tell Lucia make the Don's breakfast."

"No," Carlo rejected firmly. "I wish now to go to the chapel. We'll wait for Father Marchesi. Afterward, I'll have breakfast."

"Giuseppe, where is Andrea?" Mama asked, and I quickly drained my coffee cup, gearing myself to meet Carlo Mazzini.

"At breakfast, Signora," Giuseppe—the omniscient—reported. "You want I call her?"

"No." Mama's voice carried distinctly to me. "Tell her I will be all morning with my son. No reading. This is a beautiful day—say she is to walk about the grounds, lie in the sun, read. At lunch she will meet the Don."

"How is the girl?" Carlo asked, and my heart pounded as I eavesdropped.

"A jewel." But Mama sighed heavily. "Carlo, I told you before—I tell you now. Is wrong to bring her here!"

The quick silence in the corridor told me Carlo was cautioning his mother against my overhearing. In the breakfast room, I gripped tightly at my coffee cup, stared at the circlet of black at the bottom. Mama

Mazzini knew someone wished me ill. The note would hardly astonish her. *She knew who was to blame*. Why did she allow him—or her—to remain at the castle?

I forced a smile, a look of preoccupation when Giuseppe came into view. With his usual air of faint annoyance, he reported Mama Mazzini's exhortations.

"Thank you, Giuseppe." Did Giuseppe agree with Mama, that I shouldn't be here? Did he, too, know why? Sometimes, behind the stern demeanor, I felt that Giuseppe lived in a permanent fearfulness.

Lucia puttered in, poured a third cup of coffee, ignoring my weak resistance. I wished, again, that Suzy were within phoning distance, that Dad was alive and available to advise. But Dad would never run from trouble, I reminded myself. He had a reputation for following through many a dangerous assignment in his lifetime, never allowing himself to be frightened away. Where there was a principle involved, Dad was immovable. I think this was the trait I most admired in him. It had been good to be able to admire as well as love my father. It wrought an unusual closeness between us.

Nostalgically, I finished my coffee, went down the corridor into the sitting room with the double doors which led to the terrace. The sun streamed across the wrought-iron, colorfully upholstered, elegantly modern garden furniture. Surprisingly, the New York *News*—only one day late—lay, disheveled, across a table. Nino must have been reading out here earlier. Checking that Aldo left on time to arrive at the airport as prearranged. Some of Nino's arrogance retreated in the presence of his uncle. Maybe with Carlo Mazzini here, Nino would leave, I thought hopefully.

I lay back on the chaise, relishing the splash of sun on my face. Too uptight to scan the tabloid that sprawled close by, though normally I eagerly read any New York newspaper. Suzy and I felt ourselves marvelously sophisticated because we subscribed to the *Village Voice*.

I was fighting a losing battle to pretend—even to myself—that I was unaware that Antonio's grandson had moved further down in the side garden. He was working absorbedly now among the bushes of red and pink peonies. He glanced up, perhaps feeling the weight of my gaze. He spied me. Waved casually, in memory of that brief encounter at the gates. The gesture was heartening. On impulse, I rose to my feet, strolled in his direction. Self-conscious, yet moving compulsively to where he worked.

"How's your grandfather?" I called out casually as I approached him.

"He'll be all right," Tony reassured quickly. "He has these arthritic attacks every now and then. Painful but not serious," he explained, his eyes, his smile, warm with friendliness. "It usually means we're in for a spell of rotten weather."

"He's a sweet man," I said softly. "And so very proud of you."

Tony chuckled.

"My grandson, who goes to college," he mimicked tenderly. "Of course, the way I do it, it's taking a long time. Seven years so far," he admitted. "Before this last year, I took a whole year off to earn money, worked like a dog down in New York, where the money is better than it is up here." He grinned reminiscently.

"How do you like New York?" How difficult to remain casual, this close to him!

"Some things about New York are fabulous," he conceded. "The museums, the libraries, the restaurants. I found a place in the Village that made spaghetti—hmmm!" He gestured eloquently. "I could close my eyes and believe it was my grandmother's!" He continued to work while we talked. I caught the note of caution in his eyes as they scanned the scenery. He wasn't being paid to entertain me. "When I got homesick for the land, I went to Bronx Park."

"I lived in New York from the time I was fourteen until I was almost seventeen," I reported, those years suddenly upon me with kaleidoscopic colorfulness. Dad was away a lot, but when he was home we were together every possible moment. "On my birthday Dad used to take me down to McDougal Street for Veal *Parmigiana*. We had a cook in Sicily," I remembered, "who made the best *Parmigiana* in the whole world."

"You lived in Sicily?" His eyes were appraising.

"We went there because Dad was working there," I explained. How good it felt, to be standing here talking with Tony. It was difficult to believe this was Antonio's grandson. But Tony was my generation, lived in my world—not Antonio's. There was a two-generation gap. Mentally, Antonio was back in his hill town home of Sicily—Tony was the now scene. "Being able to speak Sicilian got me the job here. I read to Mama Mazzini—" I halted, momentarily abashed at using the familiar term but Tony accepted it as routine, "I read to her while she waits for surgery on her eyes." But Tony knew, of course. Every drop of news about the castle must be brought home by Antonio.

"My grandfather told me," Tony acknowledged. "That makes you special in his eyes. He told me, also, that you're beautiful, like the northern Italians . . ."

"Have you ever been to Sicily?" Suddenly, I was self-conscious before the blatant admiration in his eyes.

"I never got down that far, not below Florence," he said, and hesitated at my look of astonishment. "I know—it's heresy not to go to the family home. But all I could afford was one of those fourteen-day packaged tours. Three years ago, this was," he said reminiscently. "We hit the major cities—that was the bit. Still, it was a great trip. I starved all through the school year after that—but it was worth it."

"The castle is beautiful, isn't it?" I said with forced

lightness because the chemistry was bubbling over between us again.

"Beautiful from the outside," he agreed.

"Fantastic inside," I insisted, my eyes glowing.

"I've never been inside," Tony said wryly. "No stranger—except for Father Marchesi, and now you—" he grinned infectiously, "ever sets foot inside Castle Mazzini. Not even my grandfather who has worked here since the construction was finished ten years ago —and he's a *paisan*. At five sharp each afternoon Grandpop checks out at the gatehouse. If he's busy and forgets the time, Rico calls up to the castle, and Aldo or Giuseppe comes out to tell him." Tony shrugged incomprehension.

"It must have taken a long time to put up the castle," I said with curiosity, my eyes inquiring. Why was Antonio hustled off the castle grounds sharply at five? Did Tony know about the patrol? That Rico was armed? Yet I knew I mustn't gossip with Tony about the castle routine—this would be unforgivable. "It was a fantastic job to accomplish."

"It took close to four years. Carlo Mazzini had a heart attack about fourteen years ago, the way I've heard the story told." How old was Tony? Twenty-three or twenty-four, I guessed. "Right after the heart attack, he decided to build the castle for the old lady. The whole village was agog. There were some people," Tony admitted somberly, "who were against the whole scene. It turned them off to see something so costly going up in an area where a ten thousand dollar house was considered a fine achievement. Also, there aren't many Italians in the county—intolerance puffs up its ugly head from time to time." Suddenly, I noted the guarded look in Tony's eyes. "Take these to the Signora," he directed, almost formally, and snipped swiftly at a cluster of lush pink peonies. "My grandfather says she's partial to this bush."

"Thank you."

I smiled perfunctorily, my voice as impersonal as I could contrive. Knowing that someone from the castle

must be close at hand. Watching us. I accepted the
flowers, swung about, to face the quizzical eyes of
Aldo, about twenty feet away. Nino would be told
that I'd been talking to the handsome young gardener.

I went into the castle with the peonies, sought out
a vase, then asked Rosa to take them up to Mama
Mazzini's rooms. I knew she'd be in the chapel all
morning.

"*Bello*," Rosa grunted, and trotted off with Tony's
offering of showy pink peonies.

Luncheon was served late, with much extra activity
in setting it up. Because the Don was here, I
gathered from the excited voices. Sophia and Giuseppe arguing about the tablecloth to be used. Lucia
putting in her recommendation for dishes.

Giuseppe came to me, where I sat reading in the
small salon. I had an aversion to returning to my
rooms at this point, with the note still tucked away,
unread by anyone other than myself, in my slacks
pocket.

"Signorina, lunch will be served in a few minutes."
He bowed stiffly, and hurried off.

Fighting self-consciousness, I put down the magazine I'd been trying to read, headed for the dining
room. The others were there already, I gathered.
Evidently, Father Marchesi was lunching with us. I
could hear him in conversation with Carlo Mazzini.

When I entered the dining room, the table re-
splendent with the finest dishes and most exquisite of
Mazzini glassware, Carlo Mazzini was positioning his
mother at the foot of the table. I understood. When
he was present at the castle, Carlo sat at the head.

I had expected Carlo Mazzini to be a tall, brawny
man, similar to Nino in proportion. He was small,
compactly built, with closely cropped near-white hair
and a salt-and-pepper beard, meticulously trimmed.
When his eyes swung from Father Marchesi to me, I

felt their impact. Piercing brown eyes, which would miss nothing.

"Andrea," Mama called to me with affection. "Come, meet my son and Father Marchesi."

Carlo Mazzini, with an Old World courtliness, switched on his considerable charm while Mama Mazzini introduced me. The four of us settled ourselves at the table—where was Nino?—and exchanged polite, impersonal conversation. I knew that Carlo Mazzini was making his own personal assessment of me, even as I was doing of him. An air of great strength about him—and something else, indefinable at the moment. I could understand the atmosphere of respect, of caution, that emanated from the servants when they spoke of the Don. This would be a valuable friend, a formidable enemy.

"Your parents are visiting Europe, I understand?" Carlo said with warm interest. "Their first trip?"

"Oh, no—" My impulse was to correct the small, white lie about my parents. But that would be embarrassing to Dean Benedict. "My father's business takes him to Europe for long periods of time." Was Carlo Mazzini testing me? The suspicion leaped into my mind, taking me by surprise. Carlo Mazzini knew I'd lived in Sicily! Or had someone else in the family made the arrangements for my being here? Here I was jumping to conclusions again, I chastised myself. "I lived in Sicily for three years," I picked up. "Palermo, Messina, Catania for a while . . ."

"Ah, yes, my brother told me." His smile apologetic. "I was born not many miles from Catania."

He *had* been testing me, my mind insisted. Carlo Mazzini was the kind of man who would be furious to discover someone had lied to him about credentials. I had lived in Sicily—no lie there.

Nino joined us just as Giuseppe arrived with the antipasto, Giuseppe himself serving on this special occasion, with Sophia—wearing a broad smile—trailing behind as his assistant. Father Marchesi and Nino flanking Carlo. I sat, as usual, at Mama's right.

But I realized I was viewing everyone with suspicion. Because of the note shoved under my door. *Who had put it there? Why?*

I tried to relax, to join the table conversation. Father Marchesi was deferential to Carlo, tender to Mama Mazzini. I sensed he was surprised at my presence at the castle. Nino was subdued in the presence of his uncle.

Could it have been Nino who put the note there, out of annoyance at my rejection of him? No, that didn't make sense. But the note itself didn't make sense!

Out in the kitchen, we could hear Lucia importantly scolding Rosa.

"Quick, the special cups! The Don is here!"

While I chatted with Mama about the peonies Tony had sent her, and she was expressing condolences for Antonio's arthritis attack, I saw Carlo take a slip of paper from his pocket, hand it to Father Marchesi, who was effusive in his thanks. A contribution to the church, I gathered, in recognition of today's special service. Nino was grinning smugly. I could read his mind, relishing the power of money.

While we were at coffee, Giuseppe came in to whisper into Carlo's ear.

"Nino, a phone call," Carlo reported, when Giuseppe straightened up. "You take it. It's from Las Vegas. Today I don't talk business." Yet I intercepted the exchange between Carlo and his nephew. If this were an emergency—urgent—he would talk.

"I'll go talk to them," Nino agreed, his eyes traveling arrogantly to me, as though to show off his importance in the Mazzini business empire.

"Mama, tell me," Carlo turned to his mother with infinite affection. "What can I have sent up from New York to make you happy?"

"You, Carlo," Mama chortled. "You make me happy."

"How would you like to have Victor up here for a week or two?" he demanded archly.

Mama's face lighted.

"Carlo, here? But his foot?"

"His foot is in a cast. He walks with it," Carlo said triumphantly. "I spoke with his mother yesterday. In a couple of days, he may be able to come up here."

"Ah, it is always a beautiful day when my Victor comes to see me." Mama beamed. "But do not let him come without the doctor saying it is all right," she cautioned. "Maybe now," she went on with sly demureness, "with Victor at the castle, you will send Nino off to where he is more useful."

Carlo laughed deeply.

"Mama, you have a silent vendetta with Nino. For no reason at all," he reproached.

"Carlo, how you say this?" But Mama's smug smile said she didn't mind transmitting this message to her eldest son. "My brother's grandson . . ."

"Nino is loyal—he works hard," Carlo began, and Mama snorted with a lack of delicacy that brought a smile to Father Marchesi's face. "Nino is important to the family," Carlo continued vigorously, but his eyes were wary. "Victor is not interested in working with his grandfather. It's useless to try to talk to him—" I was curious before the enigmatic exchange between Mama and Carlo.

"Victor is not for the business," Mama said tightly.

"I know—" Frustration colored Carlo's voice. A kind of incomprehension. "My grandson is all concerned about blacks in Harlem and Indians on the reservations. For this he had to go to a fancy law school?" Sarcasm laced his voice.

"He is young, my Victor." Mama's face took on a command that brought out, unexpectedly, a sharp resemblance to her eldest son. "Let him find himself."

So Mama's favorite, Victor, would be arriving at the castle. I turned this over in my mind, burning with curiosity. I could feel an affinity for someone concerned about blacks in Harlem and Indians on the reservations. Also, the arrival of another Mazzini male would put restraints on Nino.

When we were done with Lucia's sumptuous luncheon, Carlo walked Father Marchesi out to his car. Giuseppe wheeled Mama back to the elevator, escorted her upstairs for her afternoon nap. All of the lunch-time conviviality had evaporated from Mama. She would lie in bed and think about her dead son, I thought compassionately. Two sons dead, I remembered. What pain it must be to lose two sons.

Alone again, I was restless, recurrently conscious of the ugly note that nestled in the pocket of my slacks. Who in this castle had framed that message, slid it beneath my door? I churned with a need to confide in someone. Not to hold this warning in solitude. Yet I realized now I mustn't disturb Mama Mazzini. Not today.

I hovered uncertainly on the terrace, fighting down a compulsion to share the note with Tony. No, I was out of my mind! How could I talk to a complete stranger—a gardener on the property—about something like this? And I'd have to watch myself, not make myself conspicuous by knuckling to my inclination to walk wherever Tony was working and talk with him.

I dropped onto the chaise, stared out at the lush summer greenness. The sun was hiding behind the clouds now. We seemed to be in for a summer shower. I could hear Father Marchesi driving down the roadway to the public road. Carlo Mazzini was walking back into the castle. There, the door was closing behind him.

On impulse, I leaped to my feet, crossed the terrace, hurried through the room that led to the corridor. Carlo Mazzini saw me, smiled.

"Well, Andrea," he said expansively, "how do you like living here at the castle?" Pride in his eyes as they swept the richly ornate corridor.

"It's wonderful, Mr. Mazzini," I said quietly, and reached into my slacks pocket to pull forth the note. "But evidently someone in the castle doesn't want me here . . ."

His face was instantly alert, guarded. His dark eyes opaque as he reached for the note. I watched somberly while he read, feeling the silent rage in him.

"Andrea, don't worry about this—this piece of stupidity," he said calmly, yet I knew his inner fury. "I will handle this. Now, Andrea," he smiled, seeming to dismiss the threat against my life. "Now, will you do a special favor for me?"

"If I can." Relief surged through me because Carlo Mazzini knew, and was angry.

"I'll tell Aldo to drive the car around, to take you into the village." I refrained from saying I could drive myself, if he'd allow me to take one of the cars in the garage. "There is a shop there—Aldo will point it out—which handles many fine chocolates. Choose a mixture for my mother. About a pound." His eyes softened, acquired a glint of amusement. "More candy than that in the castle and she'll eat herself sick."

"Shall I go right away?" I accepted the bill he extended, realizing he wished me out of the way while he sought out the culprit. I could understand this. It would be an ugly scene.

"Right away, please," he said with charming courtliness. "I'll tell Aldo to bring the car out front. And don't worry, Andrea—this absurdity will stop."

From the cold glint of anger in his eyes, I believed—then—that it *would* stop.

CHAPTER

6

I thrust the bill Carlo Mazzini had given me into the slacks pocket which had, until moments ago, held the block-lettered threat to my life. I strolled out to the front of the castle to wait until Aldo drove around for me. He appeared surprisingly fast. Not one of the black limousines apparently most favored at the castle, but a gleaming, red Mercedes Benz, upholstered dramatically in black. Even Aldo seemed less sullen behind the wheel of this car.

Silently, I climbed into the rear, settled back. Aware of furtive glances in the rear-view mirror as we drove along the narrow, winding country roads. Aldo was curious about my going into the village.

"This is a gorgeous car," I said finally, to break the heaviness of the silence between us. Oh, I would have loved to be behind the wheel of this car!

"*Si*, Signorina," he agreed, and abandoned the furtive glances in the mirror.

The village was at least nine miles from the castle. The houses were small, unpretentious. There was a rather new, quite lovely Catholic church, which I gathered must be Father Marchesi's. I would bet that the Mazzini family figured heavily in its endowment. An ancient but neatly tended white clapboard Baptist church, with a plaque announcing its date of establishment as 1756, occupied a corner at what was apparently the business section of the village. One block of shabby stores—the sort you see in a depressed area —with the single exception of a modern combination

71

drug and candy store. Freshly painted, with black
wall-lamps flanking its attractively molded door, its
windows carrying eye-catching displays that seemed
more city than village. The store sat there like a
prize-winning rose in a garden of weeds.

I pulled open the door, recognizing the country-
rare air-conditioning, walked into the immaculate,
surprisingly large store. A short, heavy, smiling man
in a white apron crossed from the sparkling drug
section to the neat rows of candy display cases toward which I was walking.

"Nice day," he said, his accent distinctly Italian. I
noticed that his eyes were focusing on the red
Mercedes at the curb. He realized I was from the
castle. Who else in this town would own a Mercedes?
His smile warmed. I was, obviously, a special cus-
tomer.

We talked casually about the weather as I made
my choice from the display cases—a mixture, as Mr.
Mazzini had ordered. The man scooping up candy
with such care in the small aluminum shovel was
proud of his shop.

"Everything looks so delicious," I said, accepting
the sample candy, a new variety, which he insisted I
taste.

"I try to please." He shrugged. "Eight years I've
been here—but to the people here," his eyes were
scornful, "I'm still a newcomer. They buy from me,"
He gestured expressively. "I'm the only drugstore in
town—they used to have to drive miles. But we're still
the folks who came up from New York. Is lonesome
sometimes, for my wife and me. The children all
married, living down on Long Island. Every time
they manage, they come up. With the grandkids.
Eleven," he pronounced with rich satisfaction.

With the candy arranged in an attractive box,
wrapped in white-and-gold striped paper, I reached
for the bill in my pocket, pulled it forth.

"No, no!" He brushed this aside as though it were an

absurdity. "For Mama Mazzini, no charge. My pleasure." He was nodding in effusive affirmation.

From the corner of my eye, I saw the rotund wife emerge from the rear as I headed for the door. She began to argue volubly—in Italian—with her husband, while both stared at the Mercedes. She was angry. She hated the Mazzinis! Yet her husband had insistently refused payment for candy for Mama Mazzini.

I climbed back into the Mercedes. Wordlessly, Aldo pulled away from the curb, swung about in a U-turn to take us back to the castle. I leaned back in the car, staring absently at the beauty of the mountains rising ahead of us. But the furious face, the matching voice, of the drugstore owner's wife lingered uncomfortably in my mind.

Aldo deposited me in front of the castle, drove off to garage the car. My heart was pounding while I waited for someone to open the always locked door, in response to my ring. What had happened in my brief absence? Had Carlo Mazzini sought out—and found—whoever threatened my life in that ugly, blunt fashion? I wished, fervently, that he had.

The door was pulled wide. Sophia smiled at me, noticing the candy box I held.

"Please go to the library, Signorina," Sophia ordered importantly. "The Don is waiting for you there."

"Thank you, Sophia." But I was uncertain. Which was the library?

Sophia read my mind.

"I show you, Signorina," she offered. "This way."

I followed Sophia to a pair of large double doors at the rear of the corridor. One of the doors stood wide. I stared inside uncertainly.

The library appeared to be a conference room as well. Every wall, except the fireplace wall, was lined to the ceiling with books, most of which wore an air of being seldom opened. The ceiling was vaulted, painted with *di sotto in sù* frescoes. A huge, oval table flanked by modern armchairs, upholstered in black leather, monopolized the room. A pair of black leather armchairs sat at right angles to the fireplace, and at one corner was placed an executive-type desk, with a portable electric typewriter incongruously sitting at one side.

Carlo Mazzini, wearing heavy, tortoise-shelled glasses, sat in one of the chairs by the fireplace. He was reading what appeared to be a lengthy contract.

"Mr. Mazzini," I said softly, at the door.

He glanced up quickly, smiled, laid aside the contract.

"Please, come in, Andrea." He reached out a hand for the gift-wrapped box. "Mama will be pleased with her treat," he said leisurely, his eyes cautiously scanning the doorway, though we both knew Mama Mazzini would be in her rooms till dinner.

"The man at the store absolutely refused to take money," I said, handing him the bill.

"Mario is a good man." Carlo chuckled indulgently. "Once, I did a small favor for him. He never forgets." But Mario's wife had been furious, I recalled. "Andrea," Carlo Mazzini lowered his voice. "That matter we discussed. Nothing like this will happen again. I promise you. The idiot who left that note in your rooms is retarded, a servant—we keep him here because he is a distant relative. But he realized he was suspected. He has run away. He's probably across the Canadian border by now."

"Thank you." I smiled my relief.

I left him, went upstairs to my rooms. Opening the door, I started when my eyes spied the small blue envelope which stared up at me from the floor. I reached to pick it up, smiled ebulliently. An airmail from Suzy. Lovely!

Suzy knew where I was, of course. It would be impractical—impossible—for me to try to answer her, the way she was hopping from city to city, country to country. We hadn't bothered to figure out her itinerary by date. I wished, wistfully, that we had.

I dropped into a chair to read, eagerly, the brief hastily scrawled airmail. Suzy was having a ball—she hoped my summer was working out well. It would, after this, I promised myself.

I scanned my collection of paperbacks, chose a mystery that had been especially recommended. I'd settle myself out on one of the balconies off my rooms. Tiny, just large enough to hold one garden chaise.

I pulled open the tall casement windows that led to the balcony, slid myself into the chaise, opened the book at the first chapter. I saw the words. I tried to concentrate. But nothing was sinking in. I was astonished to discover I was still uptight. Carlo Mazzini had assured me there'd be no repetition of that incident. *The perpetrator had run away.* I'd accepted that, hadn't I? Mentally, yes. Emotionally, no.

This was ridiculous, I upbraided myself. Relax! But despite my efforts, my eyes refused to focus on the pages before me. Instead, I found myself surveying the grounds below. Where was Tony working?

Oh, I must stop this! How could I develop a hang-up so quickly? Because of the isolation—that was the reason. I was striving to be realistic. I missed the easy companionship of the campus. The full social life. Before college, we'd lived in the city. I wasn't accustomed to being cut off from people this way. Of course, I was drawn to Tony!

But I tensed into alertness when I spied Tony, back at the front of the garage. What was he doing? Inspecting that impressive array of cars. He probably flipped for the red Mercedes, I guessed with a flicker of humor.

Tony was being cautious—he kept glancing about, with an eye for the approach of Aldo or any of the other servants. He must see someone, the way he was straightening up now, strolling away, back to the wheelbarrow sitting beside one peony bush.

I strived, again, to dig into the mystery across my lap. Normally, I relished a solid chunk of time in which to sit and relax with a book. Today, too much churned about in my mind. Religiously, my gaze wandered to where Tony was working. I was relieved—and disappointed—when he moved on to another area, beyond my view.

I wondered if dinner would be served as early as usual, with Carlo Mazzini at the castle. Assuming that it would, I changed from slacks into my one "little black dress," hung a silver chain, which had been Dad's last birthday gift to me, around my neck. Like the others at the castle, I was conscious that the Don's appearance here was a special occasion.

I left my rooms, started down the corridor, my footsteps muffled by the lush carpeting. And then I froze—fleetingly—at the sound of voices behind a door near the head of the stairs.

"Uncle, I tell you it was a mistake!" Nino was saying urgently. Up to this moment, I hadn't been sure which rooms were Nino's. "A mistake to bring that broad here!"

"What's the matter, Nino?" Carlo mocked in annoyance. "This girl won't let you near? Go home for a day. Go home and see your wife. There you'll get in no trouble."

My face got hot, I moved swiftly down the wide, circular staircase to the lower floor. Why was it a mistake to bring me here? Had Carlo Mazzini lied about the retarded servant who was probably "across the Canadian border by now"?

Dinner, as I'd anticipated, was a sumptuous feast. The men ate with obvious enjoyment. Giuseppe moved about the table with a variety of wines. Mama's eyes seldom left her son's face, even while she talked to me about her early days in this country, as a bride. Days so in contrast to the family's present great wealth.

Immediately after dinner, a lengthy affair this evening, Carlo returned with Mama to her rooms. I hurried quickly to my own rooms, though I doubted Nino would start up with his uncle at the castle. Still, the glances he'd shot in my direction when Carlo and Mama Mazzini had been talking absorbedly to each other across the dining table had disturbed me. Nino couldn't conceive that anything female might find him repulsive.

The evening was unusually warm for the mountain area. I crossed to open the windows, first in my sitting room, then in the bedroom. At the last window, I stood drinking in the night air, fragrant with the blend of flowers, recently mown grass, peppermint and clover. Pleasantly cool in contrast to the indoors. On impulse, I decided to sit out on the balcony for a while.

Only a sliver of moon was visible, but the sky was clear, generously splashed with stars. How strange, to be sitting here alone on this balcony, at this hour of the evening! But then, I mocked myself humorously, if I were working at that day camp, I'd be too pooped at night for anything except sleep.

My gaze settled on the man moving slowly about the grounds below. The night patrol. Distaste for such security brushed at me. Had Carlo Mazzini lied to me about the threatening note? He'd seemed so positive— how could I question a man like that? Yet, I'd heard that exchange between Nino and Carlo. *Had Carlo lied to me?* How would I know? I shivered. If he'd lied, I'd know.

"Everything is going well," Carlo's voice, touching off excitement in me. Talking complacently to someone below. I leaned back in the shadows, not wishing to be seen. "As I expected."

"When?" Nino demanded avidly. "When will we go into operation?"

Carlo chuckled.

"Don't be greedy, Nino. Soon enough. We will hold the meeting soon. I'll give you warning. Top security, Nino—you know the importance of this, for all of us. The merger must be fully completed before the word leaks out."

The two men were walking toward the garage. Carlo carried an attaché case. He was leaving the castle tonight, I suddenly realized. The lights had been switched on in the garage, One of the long black Cadillacs was driving out into the night.

I was suddenly chilly. I went inside, closed the window. I was probably kooky to wonder about Carlo Mazzini's truthfulness. He was the kind of man who wouldn't tolerate such goings on at the castle. If he said the man was gone, then the man was gone.

Inside again, I was restless. Mama Mazzini had ordered a TV set installed in my room. The reception up here was magnificent. For a few minutes, I tried to become involved in a television program. My attention strayed morbidly.

What did Tony do for amusement, down in the village where he lived? What diversion was available? The local ginmill? I hadn't seen even a movie in town, though there must be a drive-in servicing the area.

I sighed heavily. Oh, it was going to be a long, lonely summer! Face up to this. Unless some social life developed with Tony, which—at this point— appeared unlikely. Yet it was hardly a way-out idea, I considered with an effort at casualness. We were close in age—he must be no more than three or four years older than I. We were both going into our last year at college. We'd both lived in New York. We had a lot in common.

If Tony should make a suggestion—dinner in town or a movie—I wouldn't turn him down, I promised myself defiantly. Would he feel uncomfortable because he was working here as a gardener and I was sort of a paid guest? That would be a square attitude! Square Tony wasn't.

If he asked me out, I'd go. *If* he asked me. I hoped that he would.

With Carlo Mazzini gone, the household settled down into its normal routine. Except that Nino was increasingly restless. Nights, he played the color TV so loudly that Mama muttered under her breath. Or he prowled the grounds, talking noisily with the man on patrol. Later in the evening, he usually took one of the cars and drove off with a shriek of brakes, probably to the nearest ginmill.

I sensed that Nino was annoyed at being kept here at the castle while an important merger was being formed. Perhaps, Carlo wanted Nino—the gauche—out of the way, I considered with sardonic humor. I knew the deep familial ties of the Sicilians, yet Carlo Mazzini would hardly consider Nino an asset in high-level business negotiations.

Antonio's arthritis was keeping him in bed. Each day I solicitously inquired of Tony—and lingered to talk casually. About campus unrest, about New York, about the ghetto outbreaks in cities across the country. We were *simpatico*, both pleased by this. Yet, I chafed before an inner wariness in Tony that prohibited his putting our relationship on a social, boy-girl basis.

By the time Tony was completing his fifth day as substitute for his grandfather, and Mama was offering to send over her personal physician, whom she considered a miracle-worker, I felt as though I'd known Tony for years. Knowing none of the minute details of his life, but the way he thought.

I sat on the terrace, while Mama Mazzini took her long, afternoon rest, and pretended to be absorbed in the fashion magazine that lay open across my lap. Aware that in a few moments Tony would check his watch, realize it was almost five, and begin to pack up for the day. Tony was scrupulous about checking out on the dot of five. Neither before or after. Five sharp.

I thought about Mama at lunch yesterday, when she'd offered to send Aldo on a seventy-mile trip both ways to bring Dr. Lucas to examine Antonio and prescribe. Mama had been furious at Nino's snide

attitude. She'd chewed him out in a rich flow of rapid
Sicilian, and he'd sullenly back-tracked.

Nino was arrogant, yes, but protective of his place
in the Mazzini hierarchy. His by birth rather than
ability, I strongly suspected. It was difficult to conceive of Nino as having the financial wizardry to
merit a half-million dollar home in Westchester.

I straightened into alertness. Tony was stowing
away his tools in the wheelbarrow. He'd be leaving in
a few minutes, to go back to his house in the village.
It was strangely difficult for me to envision Tony in
that house.

This morning, when we'd been talking, Tony said
his grandfather was improving. Antonio could be returning any day, I warned myself wistfully. And Tony
would go back to working in the fields.

I watched Tony leave the grounds, stride lithely
into the walled avenue to the gates. Out of sight.
Restless now, I dropped the fashion magazine on the
coffee table, rose to go into the castle. Go upstairs,
freshen up for dinner.

In the corridor, I ran headlong into Nino and was
startled by the impact of his massive body. He caught
me by the shoulders, steadied me.

"Where's the fire?" Nino jibed, grinning smugly.
Enjoying this physical encounter.

"I'm sorry," I apologized, faintly breathless, stiffen-
ing defensively before the arousal in his eyes.

"I'll let you make up for almost knocking me
down," he drawled, one hand closing possessively
about my arm. "When the old lady's tucked away for
the night, I'll take you for a long, moonlight drive—"

"No thanks!" I flashed back.

His eyes darkened, ugly with rage. His hand was
bruising hard on my arm.

"You wouldn't say that if that creepy gardener
asked you!" he taunted. "Antonio's grandson wouldn't
get a 'no' like that!"

"Tony doesn't have a pregnant wife," I reminded
him, suddenly trembling yet thinking clearly. Give

Nino's sick ego an out, my mind warned. "Now let me go," my eyes holding his, refusing to back down. "Let me go," I repeated, more firmly. My eyes warning, now, that I'd yell for Mama Mazzini if he didn't.

With a brutal suddenness, he released me.

"Go," Nino said contemptuously. "Who needs you?"

Shaking from the encounter, I hurried up the stairs. Nearly tripping halfway up in my haste to remove myself from Nino, my heart thumped while I clutched at the banister for safety. What an obnoxious man! I'd hoped to avoid an actual confrontation, such as this, with Nino. Absurdly, I was upset.

I was relieved to be within the privacy of my own rooms. To be busy with the small business of changing for dinner. I'd adopted this habit because I sensed that Mama appreciated this nicety. My wardrobe was not actually lavish, I mocked myself as I chose the last dress as yet unworn at the castle.

It was too early to go downstairs for dinner. I hardly relished the prospect of running into Nino again, without the protective presence of Mama Mazzini. Dressed now, I flipped on the television set just moved into my green-and-gold sitting room, subconsciously thinking how incongruous this modern entertainment device was in this 1750 castle. With a program filling the generous-sized screen, I dropped onto the small sofa, kicked off my shoes and tucked my feet beneath me.

My eyes were fastened on the screen. My thoughts roamed. I noted the spot on my arm which was sure to be a small, ugly bruise tomorrow. Nino Santini's print marks, I thought with distaste. Don't think about that. Try to find another program.

I moved to the TV set, fiddled with knobs, then impatiently flipped off the viewing button, in no mood for such diversion. I crossed to the window, stared out at the late afternoon sunlight. Why didn't Nino leave the castle?

Nino wouldn't start trouble for Tony, would he? I wasn't apt to underestimate that crack about Tony.

Oh, why was it so important to the Mazzinis that a male member of the family be in residence? Because of Mama's age, my mind probed with a sudden flow of compassion? So that there was no possibility that Mama Mazzini might die alone, among servants? Wow, I was morbid!

All right, go on downstairs, I pushed myself. I ran a brush over my hair, not that it was really necessary, took a deep breath, and started for the door. I walked out into the corridor, down to the staircase with a new caution stirring in me. Silent war between Nino Santini and me now—nobody had to remind me of this. It was a disquieting realization.

A smile touched my face. That faint whirr of a motor sounded beautiful! Mama Mazzini, en route to the dining room, via her private elevator.

Dinner, as always, was a gourmet masterpiece. Tonight, I ate with painful constraint. Too conscious of the seething anger in Nino, who sat on the other side of Mama. Mama sensed there had been some encounter between Nino and me. I saw the concern on her face as—with her clouded vision—her eyes swung from Nino to me, back to Nino again. Mama realized the sullen anger festering within him. And she was aware of the unease in me. She sighed heavily, turned to question me about my post-college plans.

Mama and I talked with determined animation, in a silent pact to ignore Nino. At intervals, she shot reproving glances at him. He ignored us, bullishly concentrating on stowing away his gluttonish portion of pork chops in wine.

What about Nino's wife? Didn't she resent his being up here at the castle for what appeared to be—unfortunately—an indefinite period? Until the top-level business meeting that Carlo Mazzini and he had discussed. The important, hush-hush merger. Why must the meeting be held all the way up here? But I suppose, in New York, there were too many opportunities for leakage.

While Mama and I lingered over a second cup of expresso, Nino brusquely excused himself and left the table. Mama's gaze followed him. Her mouth set in annoyance. Nino was just one, dangerous shade away from overt hostility.

Giuseppe arrived to wheel Mama into the small salon, where we settled down to our evening schedule of reading. Tonight, Mama seldom asked me to stop, as was her custom, to reread a passage that dealt with names familiar to her. These small tidbits gave her rich satisfaction. But tonight she was disturbed about Nino, reluctant to complain to Carlo about her grand-nephew.

Earlier than I anticipated, Mama gestured for me to abandon the reading.

"No more reading tonight, Andrea." Her voice was querulous. Tonight she looked her eighty-five years. "Call Rosa for me, please. I am ready for bed." She gestured tiredly.

I quickly went off to find Rosa, who sat waiting in the kitchen for this nightly summons. Mama was wheeled off to her elevator. I went up to my rooms, reconciled to a solitary evening of TV, which would make no demands on my powers of concentration.

In my sitting room, I flipped on the set, for the comfort of hearing voices. With sound shattering the heavy silence, I headed for the bedroom, to change into pajamas. Where was Tony right now? I knew about the resort hotels, I conceded with ironic humor. But what about the local younger generation?

For Tony it must be especially dull, I thought, after the years of being away at college, of working in New York. Did he have a special girl? With someone special, you found no dullness.

Oh, stop thinking about Tony! After this summer, I'll never see him again. But I want to see him—for all the days of my life.

I kicked off my shoes, crossed to the bed. I folded the dramatic red-and-plum cut velvet spread, draped it across a chair. Returned to the bed, reached to fold

back the pair of summer blankets, the lilac top sheet.
Folded, and froze—

I stared in disbelief, cold with shock. A snake! A
coral snake, banded in red, white, and black,
slithered along the lilac bottom sheet. While I assimi-
lated the fact that the snake was there, its head
raised up, its tongue flicking out toward me.

I screamed, turned on my heels, ran. Panic closed
in on me. No written threat of death this time. A
living, breathing instrument of death, waiting to
spring!

CHAPTER

7

I sped into the corridor, my heart pounding, making sure the door was closed firmly behind me.

"Signorina—" Giuseppe was moving stiffly up the stairs, his face concerned. "What is it?"

"A snake!" I gasped. "In my bed! I think it's a coral." And coral snakes are deadly.

Sophia was running heavily behind him, slowed by her bulk. She paused at the foot of the stairs to catch her breath, crossed herself fearfully.

"A snake in the castle?" Sophia was wide-eyed with terror.

"It's there, on the bed," I repeated, feeling unreal. "I turned back the covers—and there it was." I shivered visualizing the raised head, the tongue flicking out toward me.

Rosa appeared from Mama Mazzini's rooms.

"What is the matter? Who screamed? The Signora is upset!"

"Tell the Signora everything is all right," I soothed shakily. "I—I thought I saw a snake in my rooms." Tomorrow, Mama could hear the truth.

"Tell the Signora I am calling Aldo. Is all right," Giuseppe said firmly, but his eyes were nervous. "Go back to her, Rosa," he ordered, faintly impatient, then turned to me. "Signorina, no one must go into your rooms."

"No one will," I promised grimly, my mind churning with questions. Who put that snake into my bed? With the nasty hope that I'd simply slide beneath the covers and be bitten! The snake couldn't have come up from the ground and bedded down on his own. "Giuseppe, perhaps you ought to call Mr. Santini," I suggested, striving to hold on to my cool. At this moment, I suddenly wanted to come face to face with Nino. With questions in my eyes. I could look at him and know, I told myself doggedly.

"He is away," Giuseppe reported, already hurrying off to rouse Aldo. "He leave after dinner, Signorina."

Sophia and I huddled there in the corridor. Sophia's eyes were galvanized to the bottom of the door, as though she expected that lethal monster to slide beneath and into view at any instant.

"Signorina, how come a snake in the castle?" Sophia asked me in a painful whisper. "How come he get in?"

"One of those crazy things that happen once in a hundred years." I forced a smile. Who had warned me about snakes coming down from the mountains? "Copperheads, rattlers—" It was Nino. "Don't be upset, Sophia—it'll probably never happen again."

Someone deliberately placed that snake in my bed—no doubt in my mind about that. To kill me—or frighten me away. Giuseppe said Nino was away from the castle, but he could have arranged this bit of ugliness before he left. He was furious at me tonight. Coldness wrapped itself about me. Furious enough for murder?

"Good thing Lucia go to her room," Sophia said. The servants, except for Giuseppe, slept in rooms over the garage. "Lucia scared to death of snakes—say they bad luck."

Sophia and I stiffened to attention as Aldo strode up the stairs, taking them two at a time. Giuseppe, winded from exertion, trailing behind.

"Nobody go in," Aldo said importantly, pulling a gun from a shoulder holster. "I kill that snake."

Aldo opened the door, closed it. The three of us waited uneasily. Rosa appeared down the corridor again, seeming anxious. Mama Mazzini had probably sent her out for a progress report.

Aldo's shoulder holster made me vaguely uneasy. Was Aldo always armed? I hadn't noticed before. But there had been no occasion for me to notice.

Sophia emitted a startled sound as the shot rang out in the other room. I smiled tensely.

"Is dead," Sophia said firmly, and crossed herself. "No worry about him no more, Signorina."

We heard Aldo's heavy footsteps coming toward us, clumping over the tiles. The door opened. He held the dead snake disdainfully in one hand. Sophia shrieked and retreated.

"He's not poison snake," Aldo said triumphantly. "But I kill. This one looks like a coral snake—he ain't. He's a Sonora Mountain kingsnake—hurt nobody." He stared interestedly. "Kinda pretty, you know."

"Take him away," Rosa ordered disgustedly. "Make me sick!"

Giuseppe went down the corridor to report to Mama Mazzini, with Rosa waddling at his heels. Sophia and Aldo—with Sophia keeping a respectful distance from the snake in his hand—returned to the lower floor, Sophia talking volubly to the smirking Aldo, who apparently categorized all females as low-grade morons.

Feeling sheepish, I opened the door to my sitting room, walked inside. Balked at going beyond, into the bedroom. I wasn't ready—not yet—to go into the room where Aldo had shot the snake.

I sat on a corner of the sofa, only now conscious that I was in my bare feet. They were cold from walking on the majolica tiles, the area not covered by the Aubusson rug. I reached down with a hand to massage warmth into my toes.

Oh, why had I screamed that way? Now, I felt disturbingly self-conscious about having created a scene. But the snake *did* appear to be a coral—and I know corals are deadly!

Could it have been Nino? But Nino—I knew this instinctively—had not shoved that threatening note beneath my door. Carlo Mazzini had been so sure the note was the work of the retarded servant, who'd run away under questioning, I'd gathered. But now this business with the snake—I had doubts about that.

I started at the light tapping on my door.

"Come in." I sat tensely, my voice higher-pitched than usual, from nervousness, I knew.

The door opened. Sophia walked in, with a pair of gaily flowered sheets over her arm.

"Signorina, I change your bed," she explained. "Aldo say do this—is not nice in there," she added delicately, seeming to understand that I hadn't as yet ventured that far.

"Thank you, Sophia." I smiled shakily. Tonight, despite the fright, I felt less a stranger in the castle.

But it was an hour before I could bring myself to go into the bedroom to prepare for the night.

I awoke late, probably because I'd fallen asleep only after hours of restless, fearful tossing. I opened my eyes to a dreary morning, a chill dampness pervading the room. I tugged at the blankets, bringing them up snugly over my shoulders—and with shattering impact the memory of last night assaulted me.

In my mind I visualized the snake—head raised, tongue flicking out at me—and felt faintly sick. I'd been so sure, at that moment, that it was a deadly coral. As I was supposed to believe.

Who had Carlo Mazzini frightened into running away? Not whoever wanted me away from the castle! The menace still hung over my head. How many more warnings would I receive? Would the next happening be a warning—or something less innocuous? *Why?* It was all so absurd!

Dress, get out of here. *Forget about last night.* I went to my closet in that enormous wall that would have coped with ten times my wardrobe, collected slacks against the rawness of the morning, crossed to my dresser for underthings, a sweater. A swift, hot shower, and I dressed, impatient to be downstairs, removed from the memory of last night.

I struggled to regain my cool as I walked down the staircase to the lower floor. Whoever was trying to frighten me away mustn't believe he—or she—was successful. Nino wouldn't be at the breakfast table, I reminded myself with mild satisfaction—one advantage of coming downstairs this late. He made a point of starting his round of phone calls about nine-thirty. I suspected that these phone calls had been contrived to make Nino feel important. As far as I could see, he was all muscle and little brain.

Sitting at the breakfast table, with coffee at my elbow, I gazed out the window at the overcast sky. Oh, don't let it rain! If it rained, Tony couldn't work. I needed the reassurance of casual, everyday talk with Tony, after last night's insanity. To bring me down to earth again, after the unreality in which I lived here.

Sophia brought me creamy scrambled eggs and exquisitely crisp bacon, hurried back into the kitchen for the hot rolls which were Lucia's specialty. A phone rang somewhere in the distance in what I believed to be the office wing of the castle. Two rings and it was quiet—Nino was there.

Unexpectedly, Mama Mazzini sent down word with Giuseppe that this morning she was tired. She would stay in her rooms until dinner. After dinner, we would read as usual.

"Is she all right?" I asked Giuseppe solicitously. She was a fragile eighty-five, I remembered.

"Sì, Signorina," Giuseppe reassured me. His eyes showed he was pleased with my concern. "Some days she is like this. The doctor say rest then. Is best."

"Thank you, Giuseppe." I smiled, reached for the coffee carafe to pour myself a second cup. Feeling at loose ends with no planned activities.

I sat there, sipping my coffee, anxiously scanning the sky. Was Tony working today? It wasn't raining yet. Probably he'd come. If I could talk to Tony about last night in the casual way we talked about things, then it would seem less horrendous.

I finished my coffee, cut out through the terrace at the side of the castle. Striving to conceal the urgency in me. What a raw chill in the air this morning!

My eyes scanned the grounds, searching for Tony. He was nowhere in sight. Disappointment rode over me in waves.

I went back into the castle, out to the storeroom to collect Victor's bike. Impatient for activity. In the kitchen Lucia was anxiously questioning Giuseppe about Mama's health while she prepared a breakfast tray.

I pushed the bike out to the pebbled path, climbed on the seat, began the circular ride to the closed avenue. My eyes searching the sky again. Relieved to see a slight breakthrough of sunlight. If I were caught in a rainstorm on the road, I'd be stranded with nothing more than a tree to hide beneath.

I pedaled slowly, thinking about Tony. Antonio would be returning any day now. Hadn't Tony told me he was much better? Then what happened with Tony and me? He was making no move toward socializing.

"Hi." Tony's voice, somewhere to my right.

I braked, gazed about, my heart pounding. There he was, on his haunches, before a low, flowering shrub.

"Hi." I sounded faintly breathless. Not from exertion.

"No reading this morning?" he jibed humorously. "My, you work hard!" His eyes were gently teasing. There was such tenderness in him, along with a thoroughly stubborn streak.

"Mama is resting today," I explained. Carefully, I sought the right words. "Maybe because of last night— I must have upset her ..." I shrugged, my eyes fastened to Tony. Waiting for a leading question because all at once I was uptight again.

"What happened last night?" Tony dumped the handrake, lifted himself to full height, smiling. But his eyes were serious.

"I made an ass of myself!" I managed a laugh. Yet I churned to know Tony's reaction to what happened. "I went to turn down my bed—and there was a snake there." He frowned sharply. I took a deep breath. "I was sure it was a coral. It looked like a coral. I screamed and ran!" Was that why Mama stayed in her rooms today? Because she was disturbed about the snake in my bed? Still fearful of harm coming to me?

"What was it?" Tony probed.

"It was a Sonora Mountain snake. Aldo killed it." I shivered in remembrance. "Scared me to death. If I hadn't been so meticulous last night about turning down my bed, I might have slid under the covers without seeing that thing. Poisonous or not—Aldo said it *wasn't*—lying next to it would have shot me through the ceiling."

"How did a snake get into your bed?" Tony stared at me incredulously. "That would take some doing."

"It was there," I said bluntly.

"Honey, I know it was," he soothed quickly, and I recognized—and relished—the mild endearment. "But I don't see any snake walking in all on his own."

"With that, Tony, I agree." I nodded emphatically.

"You having trouble with anyone at the castle?" His eyes searched mine. His voice low, uneasy.

"Nino," I admitted. "Mr. Santini. But I can't believe he'd stoop to something like that—" I smiled wryly. "Hardly his bag." Trying to sound flip because Tony was so serious.

"Santini's made a pitch?" Tony's dark eyes flashed angrily.

"He's tried," I conceded. "I told him off—he didn't take it too well. He's scared to push too hard because Mama Mazzini is watching him. I—I heard her tell him to stay away." I sighed. "I just wish he'd hurry up and leave."

"You expect him to cut out?" Tony asked.

"Not until after the meeting—"

"What meeting?" Tony asked curiously.

"Oh, some business meeting," I said evasively. Why

had I slipped that way? Nobody was supposed to know—not even me. But I actually wasn't spilling anything, mentioning it to Tony. He wasn't interested in high finance. "Someone mentioned it," I wound up self-consciously.

"Soon?"

"I think so." It was absurd for me to feel so upset about this leak. What did a high-echelon meeting at the castle have to do with Tony or me?

"Good. Then you'll be rid of Santini soon," Tony soothed, and I was relieved at his casualness. The meeting didn't mean a thing to him. He was only concerned that Nino leave me alone. "But we don't know," he continued somberly, "if it were Nino or somebody else who put that snake in your room."

"My first evening here, I was sure somebody had searched my rooms. Little things that were moved in my dresser drawers . . ."

"Did you say anything about it?"

"No. But later, there was a note under my door. A threatening note. 'Go home, Signorina. Go home or die.' I was scared, of course—I told Mr. Mazzini, when he came up to the castle. . . ."

"What did he say?" Tony asked interestedly.

"He pinned it on one of the servants," I explained, "who ran away under questioning . . ." Doubt lacing my voice.

"But now this," Tony pinpointed, squinting in thought. "Wrong guy ran away." His face suddenly became a polite, impersonal mask. "Giuseppe's watching us from the house. You'd better cut out. But Andrea," the command in his voice snapped me to attention. "Lock your door when you're in your rooms," he ordered crisply. "Okay?"

"Okay," I agreed shakily, and tried for a casual smile—for Giuseppe's benefit—before I moved on.

At the gatehouse, I made a point of indulging in banal conversation about the weather with a wary Rico. Some instinct in me urged this. Let it be seen that I didn't chat only with Tony—but with Rico as well.

I bicycled along the lushly green country road, with the sun playing an in-and-out game with the clouds. Why was Giuseppe watching Tony and me from the castle? Was he reporting to Nino? Oh, I wished Nino would leave!

I'd feel less uneasy if I could sit down with Tony, somewhere away from the castle. Talk fully with him about what was happening, with no fear of being watched. Whose business was it if I had a casual friendship going with Tony? Tony what, I asked myself humorously. I didn't even know his last name. But I knew the things that counted.

I biked about twenty minutes down the road, close enough to the village to see the Baptist church steeple, then swung about and headed back for the castle. What a shame I hadn't brought money along. I could have biked the rest of the way into the village, lunched there, shopped in the picturesque general store for some small trinkets. It would have been a change I'd relish.

Halfway back to the castle, I pulled off to the grassy earth, dismounted from the bicycle and dropped onto a huge rock nestling in the earth. Reluctant, yet, to go back to the castle. Stay here a while. Relax. No one in sight, only the elegant herd of black Angus grazing nearby.

I adjusted myself into a comfortable position, tried to interest myself in the pastoral scenery. But my mind was punctured by anxiety. A montage of the disquieting happenings at the castle raced through my memory.

I must arrange to spend some afternoons roaming about the village, casually socializing, I exhorted myself. To counteract the sense of being caught behind the walls of an armed fortress. I was out, wasn't I, I mocked at myself. Yet, in my mind's eye, I could see with shattering clarity the image of Rico—with his shoulder-holstered gun in view—refusing to allow me beyond the locked gate. Until the word had come down from the castle.

A stray dog, the same black-eye-patched character I'd encountered before, strolling over amiably. I picked up a stick, threw it. He joyfully embarked on a game of fetch with me. For a little while I lazily romped with the dog, then grew restless. I checked my watch. Oh, the morning was dragging! But I might as well go back to the castle. Find a book, read till lunch.

Mama Mazzini wouldn't be down for lunch, I recalled with a start. I didn't want to sit across the luncheon table from Nino, without Mama's protective presence. Maybe I could suggest, casually, that I have my lunch at the table near Lucia's herb garden, where Rosa and Sophia were apt to sit down to shell peas or scrape carrots. Al fresco dining, the European touch. I brightened at the prospect of escaping a solitary luncheon with Nino.

At the castle gates, I had to wait a few minutes for Rico to answer the bell. He came lumbering out of the cottage, a scowl on his face. Obviously, in no mood for chit-chat. Wordlessly, he reached forward to unlock the gates, swung them open sufficiently to allow me to enter.

"Thank you," I said coolly, and received a surly nod in return.

I pedaled up the awesome avenue, conscious of a sense of claustrophobia at being thus hemmed in. Feeling the weight of Rico's sullen gaze on me. So Rico hated the world—that was his problem.

I rode to the rear of the castle, put away the bike in the storeroom, headed down the corridor to the stairs. Rosa and Sophia were talking animatedly as they dusted and polished. The conversation froze when they spied me. Had they been talking about the snake? *Nobody* could believe that snake had climbed up into my room and into my bed. It was obvious he'd been deliberately placed there. What about Mama? What did she think?

I smiled slightly at Rosa and Sophia, determined not to appear uptight, strode past them, ascending the staircase. Dreading the moment when I must turn the doorknob and go into my rooms. Uneasily recalling Tony's exhortation—"lock your door."

Inside my sitting room, I hesitated, stared indecisively at the door. Yes, even in the daytime. Self-consciously I reached to lock the door.

My rooms had been done in my absence, of course. The bed neatly made. But on the small oriental rug beside my bed, I saw a much-scrubbed circle, where last night blood from the snake dripped when Aldo shot it. I shivered, looked away, crossed to the table where I'd stacked my summer library of paperbacks.

Downstairs again, I went out on the terrace—seldom used, I gathered, except by me. Read for an hour without really seeing, gradually becoming aware of hunger. All the exercise this morning, in the chill mountain air. I glanced at my watch. Soon, Lucia would be ready to serve luncheon.

I left the terrace, sauntered back to the kitchen. With an ingratiating smile, I asked Lucia if I might have lunch at the small table adjacent to her herb garden. The sun bathed the area in a delicate gold now.

"*Si*, Signorina."

Lucia smiled companionably, with knowledge in her eyes. She guessed I was making this request from a desire to avoid lunching alone with Nino. Lucia approved. At the same time, I read anxious questions in her dark, expressive eyes. Still worrying about the snake last night? Or was there something else? What did the others know that eluded me?

"Extra work for you," I apologized.

"No, not extra," she rejected expansively. "Sit down. I bring soon."

I settled myself at the white enamel garden table, choosing a chair that afforded a sweeping view of the woods to the rear of the property. A deer preserve, I recalled.

My eyes strayed about the grounds, subconsciously searching for Tony. Nowhere in view at this moment. Perhaps he was ensconced in some shady nook, having his own lunch.

Lucia brought me a mixed salad, rigatoni with sausage, chilled honeydew, and my usual coffee. I saw Rosa pushing a serving cart from the kitchen, and realized Nino must be having his lunch in the office wing. I hadn't credited him with enough sensitivity to wish to avoid me. But then, his ego was badly damaged.

I was finished with lunch, nursing my second cup of coffee, while Lucia tried to coax me into a second helping of honeydew—delicately sweet and chilled—when we heard the car drive up.

"Who come now?" Lucia demanded dramatically, straightening up to listen. Not that Lucia needed to worry about having sufficient food on hand to serve additional luncheon guests, I thought whimsically. She prepared enough daily to serve a rock festival gathering.

We heard Rosa at the door—excitable, talking stridently with obvious pleasure. A masculine voice greeted her warmly, joshingly. Giuseppe joined in with a vitality I'd never heard in him.

"Signor Victor!" Lucia's face lighted. "He come to see his grandmother. He such a good boy, that one!" Lucia waddled into the kitchen again, noisily banging pots about in her exuberance, preparing to greet Victor in the manner she loved best.

I recalled the snapshots of Victor which Mama Mazzini had shown to me with such pride. An intense curiosity stirred in me. I leaned forward, avid to see this favorite of Mama Mazzini's. No doubt in my mind that he would make a personal trip into the kitchen to greet Lucia.

Now I heard Sophia, hurrying down the stairs as fast as her bulk would permit. Highly vocal in her welcome for Victor.

"Poor bambino," she was wailing compassionately. "What they do to the foot?"

"It's all right, Sophia," he soothed. "I get about great. How's my great-grandmother?"

"Napping, Signor Victor," Giuseppe reported. "But I tell her you are here—better for her to see you than to sleep!"

"No, no, don't disturb her, Giuseppe," Victor cautioned. "I'm going to be around for a while—she'll see enough of me."

A warm, rich voice. I'm particularly susceptible to voices. I liked Victor's.

"Where's Lucia?" Victor was demanding. "Does she still make gnocchi like the angels?"

"Where will Lucia be, Signor Victor?" Sophia chafed affectionately. "But in the kitchen! You no eat lunch yet? Lucia be mad you do."

"I'm starving," Victor said with mock solemnity. His voice coming closer. "I'll tell her so myself."

"Signor Victor!" Lucia was throwing herself ecstatically upon him. Then she stepped back to inspect him. "Oh, the foot. The poor foot," she clucked.

"The foot is fine," he chuckled. "What have you got for the stomach?"

"You sit," Lucia chortled delightedly. "Sit in breakfast room. Lucia feed—"

"I'll sit out in the back," Victor decided, and I tensed self-consciously. "My favorite sidewalk café, Lucia."

Lucia dashed to the range, rattled pots, barked orders to Rosa and Sophia. Victor strode to the door, pausing there. Not yet seeing me. He took a deep breath, smiled. In no way physically like his grandfather—yet with the same strength in him.

"Beautiful, fresh air—you don't get that down in New York." He smiled brilliantly, enjoying this moment.

"No, you don't," I said softly.

Victor's eyes swerved suddenly, startled, to rest on me.

"Hi." I smiled uncertainly, disconcerted by the intensity of his gaze. "I'm Andrea Grant."

"I'm Victor Mazzini."

He crossed to the table, sat down. Something unreadable in his eyes. Was it disapproval of my being here? Not that. My mind computerized impressions—his eyes mirrored the kind of alarm I'd read in those of his great-grandmother, when we first met. Concern for me.

"I'm here for the summer," I said self-consciously. "To read to Mrs. Mazzini—"

"Who thought up this scene?" he demanded tautly, his eyes darkening with anger. "Who dragged you into the Castle Mazzini?"

CHAPTER

8

"Nobody dragged me." I managed a faintly reproachful laugh. "I was hired through my college employment agency. I was the only student at the school with a knowledge of Sicilian." My face was a hot pink. He was so upset. "I was offered the job—"

"This is a terrible place for anybody under seventy to spend the summer." He was striving to regain his cool. "It's solitary confinement. Absolutely no social life."

"I know." I smiled in wry acknowledgment. "But it's an awful lot less frantic than working all summer in a children's day camp. And I'd be an absolute washout as a waitress in a mountain resort." He regretted the outburst. Right this minute he was swearing at himself inwardly. But he'd meant it.

"Where do you go to school?" Victor asked.

"Harris," I told him, glad to be on less contentious ground. "It's a small school about thirty-five miles from—"

"I know Harris," he said quickly. Unexpectedly, his face relaxed. His eyes softened. "Has my great-grandmother been giving you a rough time?"

"She's magnificent," I said, with a burst of admiration. "I'm completely captivated."

"This house throw you?" Victor challenged, his expression cynical. "I look at all this opulence, and I think of families in the ghettos, on the reservations. In the Appalachians. But my grandfather—the family—they give much to others." It was a grudging effort, I

99

suspected, to concede this. "My grandfather alone supports a dozen families back in Sicily." Despite his smile, his eyes were troubled.

"I've gathered that." From what Mama Mazzini said at times. I sensed, too, that a tremendous double generation gap existed between Victor and his grandfather. A painful gap, with much love flowing between them.

"Where do you go from Harris?" Victor asked, making it seem a challenge.

Before I could answer, Lucia waddled out with another carafe of coffee, a cup for Victor. She poured for Victor, dramatically describing the lunch she was about to serve him, her eyes glowing at his expected response. She turned to me, about to pour a replacement. I shook my head.

"What about after Harris?" Victor picked up, when Lucia left us. His eyes were eloquently flattering me.

"For my master's in social service," I explained. Why had Victor been so upset about finding me at the castle? "I'll have to do it on a part-time basis, with a job to keep me going." I was annoyed with myself—why had I said that? "Columbia, I hope," I wound up briskly. I wasn't looking for sympathy because I'd run out of money.

Victor leaned forward, his face tense.

"I wish I had the guts to cut out, switch to social service," he admitted somberly. "That's where I want to be. I went into law in the first place because the family pushed for it. Every time I talk about a transfer, mass hysteria breaks out." He shrugged tiredly. "I'm so close to it, I'll probably take my degree—"

"A law degree can be useful in social service," I reminded, compassion warming my voice. I could understand Victor's frustrations. I could guess the family strength. "Remember, lawyers are so desperately needed by thousands of people who can't afford legal fees. In housing situations, frauds, accident cases—all kinds of circumstances." Obviously, Victor Mazzini would never need to earn money. Mama had said something, that her son had set up fabulous trust funds for all the grandchildren.

"I've thought about opening up a storefront office, up in Harlem or in the East Village," Victor said slowly. "I must take that route sooner or later." He grimaced in exaggerated anguish. "I can imagine the summit meeting when I make the announcement. My grandfather has a spot all set up—at least, in the works." He sighed heavily. "He's buying into some cigarette company, in bad shape. He wants to put me in there with their legal department." He was suddenly uneasy. "Andrea, forget what I said. About the cigarette company. It's supposed to be top secret."

"I didn't hear a thing," I flipped. So that was the merger I'd overheard Carlo and Nino discussing. I'd thought the Mazzini fortune was built around a line of olive oil and related products. But that kind of money reached out into all kinds of businesses, I reminded myself. And a bright tax lawyer—and I was certain Victor was bright—would be an asset.

He reached for the carafe of coffee, tried for a more convivial mood.

"Come on, Andrea, have another cup of coffee with me."

"This is my second already," I protested.

"So you'll have a third." He was already pouring. Victor Mazzini had a secret strength of his own, I suspected. And I admired him for this.

I sat there, faintly self-conscious. Absorbing the knowledge that I turned on Victor Mazzini. At sight— the way it had been for me, with Tony. If it were not for Tony, I probably would have discovered myself deeply drawn to Victor. Victor was intensely likeable. But there was Tony.

"You have to drink to keep me company while I have lunch," Victor pointed out with a grin. "I'd better have lunch, or Lucia will never speak to me again."

We sat and talked the way I might have talked with Tony, while Victor consumed a platter of Lucia's deliciously light gnocchi, an anchovy salad, and firmly refused seconds, despite Lucia's dramatic protestations about his slimness.

"What they feed you at school?" she demanded. "Skinny." She gesticulated with distaste. "The Signora no like! Skin and bones!"

"Before I leave I'll probably gain ten pounds," Victor prophesied. "And it'll be all your fault."

"I cook, you eat," she ordered. "No skinny around me."

"Lucia," he jibed affectionately, "we ought to open a huge, fancy restaurant in New York—with you as chef. People would stand in line for hours for a table."

Lucia giggled like an early teenager, brought him a plateful of almond rings, though normally Lucia looked down upon cake desserts as a crude American habit.

"Dig in," Victor coaxed me with relish. "Lucia's been stuffing me with these since I was old enough to know what cake was."

"I won't refuse," I laughed, reaching for one golden circlet. And then my laughter fizzled out, because Nino—massive, repulsive, eyes secretive—hovered at the kitchen door.

"Victor!" Nino bellowed, with a false joviality, after his eyes clashed fleetingly with mine. "Aldo told me you'd arrived. How's New York?"

"Hot," Victor reported. "That's how I got this—" He gestured to the walking cast on his foot. "Trying to run away from the heat and the pollution and the traffic. I went sailing off Fire Island with some college buddies."

"Break a foot sailing?" Nino appeared to consider this hilarious.

"How's the family?" Victor asked, a fresh reserve closing him off.

"Okay." Nino's eyes went opaque. "Gina's out at the Long Beach house now." He glanced with faint belligerency in my direction. "Finish up and come on out to the office with me. I want to talk to you."

Victor was annoyed, but keeping it under wraps.

"Sure, Nino," Victor said casually. "In five or ten minutes."

For an instant, I expected Nino to object to the delay. But he swung around heavily, disappeared into the kitchen. Victor and I could hear him talking in his familiarly arrogant manner with Lucia, who was arguing excitedly. Victor shook his head, shrugged. Nino annoyed him. But Lucia had been around too long to become genuinely upset, I evaluated.

Victor and I talked about sailing. Dad had early taught me to love the water. Victor had spent a summer in Europe, knew the little seaport towns of Sicily, which I remembered with such affection. Victor finished his coffee, pushed back his chair with a show of reluctance.

"I'd better see what Nino has on his mind before he has a stroke," Victor said, making this a small confidence between us. "See you later . . ."

Later in the afternoon, sitting out on my small balcony, I heard the delighted, affectionate sounds of welcome from Mama Mazzini as Victor showed himself in her rooms. For Mama this was the jewel of her life, though Mama disapproved, I surmised, of the thorough Americanization of Victor's mother.

"Victor, you sure it is all right for you to walk on that—that thing?" she demanded anxiously, evidently referring to his cast. "I do not understand. You break a foot—and right away you walk on it?"

"It's the new approach, Grandma," Victor said with a warmth that matched hers. "Progress!"

"Ah, progress . . ." Her voice was suddenly tired. "I have seen so much progress in my day, Victor—and what does it mean? You know how many wars I see in my day?"

"Too many, Grandma." An odd constraint in his voice now. "I don't like killing, either."

"Victor, tell me about your father." Mama's voice was more high-pitched than normal. She was upset. Was she afraid that Victor would be drawn into the Vietnam war? Or would Carlo Mazzini—with his powerful, financial empire—be able to pull strings? Somehow, I couldn't see Victor allowing that. "He has not been to see me in three months."

"You know Pop," Victor said gently. "All the time working. Mom complains, too."

I felt guilty about eavesdropping—but all the windows in Mama's rooms were open, and the sounds drifted out to my balcony. I was too comfortable, too involved in the conversation upstairs to budge.

"Soon you finish college, Victor. Fancy law degree. Nobody in the family yet a lawyer. Big plans for you, Victor." Mama joshed, yet I sensed she was prying.

"Granddad," Victor said, and then was silent.

"Your grandfather Mazzini fix things for you?" A kind of challenge in her voice now.

"He wants me to be part of a firm he's buying into," Victor said unhappily. "Some big corporation—very fancy," he kidded, using one of her favorite words, most frequently utilized with mild derision.

"Victor, you do what *you* want, you hear? You let nobody push you where you do not want to be!" Urgency laced her voice. I could visualize the vein in her throat distended, as was apt to happen when she became wrought up in a discussion. "Victor, you understand me—"

"Yes, Grandma, I understand . . ." Gentleness and affection blending with unease.

"All right, you go downstairs now while Rosa helps me dress for dinner. A dinner party when Victor is here," she said with an attempt at lightness. "But you remember, Victor—remember what I say."

I went inside now, to change for dinner, Mama Mazzini's exhortation rushing through my mind. For all the love she harbored for Carlo, she wasn't going to have him run Victor's life. For that I loved her. My father had brought me up to make my own decisions—

and to pay the penalty when I was wrong. He taught me to relish—to value—personal freedom. And for that I will be forever grateful.

I waited until the last moment to go down to dinner. This morning I'd been anxious to talk with Mama Mazzini about the snake which had appeared so mysteriously in my bed. Now I felt self-conscious about having created a scene, screaming that way, when the snake was completely harmless. But Mama would know—as I did—that the motive had been ugly.

Would Mama tell Victor about last night? Did Nino know? Had *Nino* been responsible? Uneasily, I considered the possibility that Mama would be sufficiently upset to prevail upon Carlo to send me away. I didn't want to leave the castle. I didn't want to leave *Tony*.

Mama knew about the snake. She didn't know about the threatening note, or that my room had been searched. Carlo Mazzini knew about the note. Would he learn about the snake incident? Only Tony knew the whole situation—and Tony was an outsider, who never set foot inside the castle.

Downstairs, I found Mama, Victor and Nino seated in the small salon. The two men were drinking, Nino with relish. Mama basked in Victor's presence.

"Andrea—" Mama leaned forward eagerly. "You have met my great-grandson?"

"Yes, earlier." I smiled at Victor, making a point of not meeting Nino's eyes.

"What's with dinner?" Nino demanded restlessly. "I've gotta cut out early." Nino's eyes, over-bold, grazed me. Victor saw this. His eyes glinted angrily. Mama, of course, had limited vision. "Lucia knows we eat early up here."

"Lucia will let us know when dinner is ready," Mama said sternly, her voice edged with sharpness. "Always in a hurry, Nino."

"Business," he shot back. "I'll take Aldo with me. He'll drive," Nino said importantly.

I intercepted the meaningful exchange between

Nino and Mama without comprehending. Something
to do with the merger, with buying into the cigarette
company, I guessed. Mama was annoyed that business must always be of supreme importance in the
Mazzini family.

"Signora—" Giuseppe hovered deferentially in the
doorway. "Dinner is ready."

Victor immediately went to his great-grandmother's
chair, as though it were a badge of honor to propel
the chair for her. Nino was swaggering as he strolled
alongside, yet I caught the suspicious, overt glances
that were beamed from Victor to me, back to Victor
again. Nino resented the casual friendliness between
us. I found the prospect of a jealous Nino disturbing.

Lucia outdid herself in honor of Victor's presence.
It was a multi-course meal with Giuseppe proudly
bringing forth special wines, which Nino ostentatious-
ly identified. The names of choice bottles from the
Mazzini wine cellar meant nothing to me. Golden-
colored Verdicchio, as pointed out by Nino, with the
funghi alla Salamoia—pickled mushrooms. Very dry
Bardolino with the broiled, marinated steak.

I candidly admitted to my ignorance of wines,
which Victor seconded. Even this championship of
me irritated Nino. Mama, attuned to the undercurrents at the table, deftly diverted the conversation
into safe channels.

"Victor, you are too thin," Mama reproached. He
wasn't. "You must eat."

"Grandma, a man's worth is not estimated by his
bulk," Victor teased. Instantly, a glint of animosity
glowed in Nino's eyes. Nino's bulk was impressive—to
Nino. Perhaps to Gina.

"I have to cut out," Nino announced brusquely.
"*Scusi, Zia.*" The expected deferential smile for his
great-aunt.

Curtly, Mama nodded. I noted the visual exchange
between them again. Some occult message that they
alone understood. I turned to Victor with curiosity.
Had he noticed? No, Victor was preoccupied.

With Nino gone some of the tension about the table fizzed away. I could feel myself relaxing. Giuseppe came in with coffee. I'd eaten heartily—I relished the expresso he was placing before us.

"Giuseppe, bring us *ratafia* in the small salon," Mama ordered with a small, anticipatory smile.

"Signora," Giuseppe rebuked. "Is not good for you."

"One small glass, Giuseppe," Mama coaxed. "Because Victor is here. Bring into the small salon when we have finished our coffee." She turned to me. "Andrea, do you know *ratafia?*"

"No." I smiled, waiting interestedly for an explanation.

"Is a cordial," Mama explained with satisfaction. "Made from nuts and fruits. You will like."

We finished our coffee quickly, as though in a conspiracy to leave the dining room—and the memory of Nino's oppressive presence. Giuseppe brought us our *ratafia*. I sipped experimentally while Mama watched.

"Oh, yes," I agreed effervescently. "It's great."

Rosa waddled into the room, to drape a wool stole solicitously about Mama's shoulders. Victor was at the fireplace, coaxing the kindling stashed between the logs into crackling fire. The evening was unseasonably cool. The warmth was welcome.

Now Mama ordered Victor to sit back while I scanned the current newspaper for her, flitting about at her direction to the sections which held most interest for her. Victor was amused at my fluency in Sicilian, a dark stranger to him except for key phrases that had been part of his upbringing.

"You—you are an ignoramus," Mama mocked smugly. "You do not even know your own language! Like his Mama," she went on, more gently. "Every morning to mass, but otherwise you think she not Sicilian. But your grandmother—my Carlo's wife," Mama said triumphantly, "She knows where she was born. Not forty miles from Taormina." Giuseppe appeared, indicating it was time for Mama Mazzini to retire, but she waved him away. "Not yet, Giuseppe," she rejected imperiously. "Not tonight, when Victor is here."

A few minutes later, we heard a car pull up outside the castle. The men's voices carried, muted, in the outdoor silence. Nino, Aldo, and two other men. Mama nodded knowingly as she recognized the voices, but she continued her conversation as though they were not there. Victor had listened attentively for a moment, now evidently had dismissed the new arrivals as of no importance. I suppressed my own lively curiosity. At the castle, any arrival was a break in the monotony of the daily routine.

Someone was at the door. The men moved into the foyer, talking animatedly together, though their words were not distinguishable all the way down the corridor. They were strolling down the corridor, probably en route to the office, I guessed.

We could hear the lively bustle of activity in the kitchen. The servants must have been alerted to the new arrivals, were preparing a meal. Nobody comes into a Sicilian house without being immediately fed, I thought humorously.

Giuseppe appeared again, crossed to Mama Mazzini, leaned over to speak quietly to her. She nodded somberly.

"*Scusi*, Andrea, Victor. I must greet some business visitors of the family. Stay here," she ordered. "I will not be long. You stay."

"We won't budge, Grandma." Victor gently derided her seriousness.

Giuseppe took his place behind Mama's chair, wheeled her from the room. Victor was inspecting me intently.

"When is Grandma scheduled for surgery?"

"I understand it's tentative for early September."

"And you're going to be here until then?"

"No," I acknowledged. "I leave the last week in August." I hesitated, loathing to perpetuate Dean Benedict's lie, yet finding it a simple explanation. "My parents will be returning from Europe then." Oh, how I wished they were alive, to return from Europe! "I'll want to spend a couple of weeks at home before I go back to school."

"Think you'll last that long?" I stared sharply at him, my heart suddenly pounding. "It can be deadly dull up here, after the first week or two," he admitted ruefully. "And don't expect diversion in the village. The villagers resent us, you know." His eyes were somber, introspective. "Except of course, for Mario and his wife, at the candy store."

"Oh, yes, I met them," I remembered. "I went down to shop candy for the Signora." He chuckled at my adopting the servant's form of formal address. But here in the castle, I felt—often—as though I were in Sicily.

"Andrea, if you feel it's wrong for you to stay here—" His eyes were seriously searching mine. "Don't hesitate to tell Grandma. She'll understand."

"I have every intention of staying!"

My voice sounded louder than I'd meant it to be. I felt heat stinging my cheeks. Oh, I was tired of unspoken thoughts that revolved around my welfare. Why shouldn't I stay? Who wanted me away? And why couldn't those at the castle—Mama Mazzini or Carlo—rid the place of someone so twisted as to threaten me? Not the retarded servant that Carlo talked so glibly about. I wasn't buying that.

"I'm not trying to drive you away," Victor scolded earnestly. "Grandma obviously loves having you here ..." His eyes said much more, about his own feelings toward me.

"Victor, it's a wonderful experience for me to be here." *Was* it? In view of all that was happening? I hovered on the brink of confiding in Victor. No, no, I mustn't.

Giuseppe came into the room, walking with more agility than normal. Motivated by the importance of the guests off in the office wing.

"*Scusi,*" Giuseppe apologized, and headed for a

corner liquor cabinet. "Signor Santini—the elder, your uncle," he explained to Victor, "wishes the Don's special Scotch for the Congressman."

"Go ahead, Giuseppe," Victor said drily. "So my uncle arrived, and he's entertaining a Congressman."

Victor was silent until Giuseppe had located the particular bottle of Scotch requested, and had departed with it. Victor rose to his feet, moved to poke restlessly at the logs in the fireplace, which were already providing a delightful warmth, a bright fan of color.

"If my uncle is entertaining a Congressman," he said with harsh sarcasm, "then the Congressman is in a position to render a favor. Or the Congressman is seeking campaign funds. Take your choice, Andrea."

The conversation between us grew heated as we discussed politicians in the public eye, argued about what we—our generation—expected from those in public office. Again, I relished Victor's outspokenness, his liberalism, which matched my own.

Neither of us were radicals. We believed in working within the framework of the Establishment, but we were starkly conscious of the need for change. And determined to work for that change. I understood the gap between Victor and his father, Victor and his grandfather. A gap that had been—a rare situation, I gathered—nonexistent between Dad, who was such a crusader until his death, and me.

Giuseppe wheeled Mama Mazzini back into the salon. She smiled, yet I sensed she was tired. At the same time, there was an odd exhilaration about her. Mama Mazzini never completely forgot the early days in a dirt-floored hut near Catania. Even now when she lived within the castle, Congressmen came to pay their respects to Signora Mazzini.

"Your uncle is here, Victor—Nino's father," she explained. "But there is business." She spread her hands expressively. "Always business."

"With the Congressman?" Victor's smile was cynical. Mama stared sharply at him. "Giuseppe came looking for Scotch to serve him. A special bottle."

Mama frowned. Victor's reaction disturbed her.

"The men will be talking until far into the night. You probably will not see your uncle," she said to Victor.

"I will survive," Victor shrugged.

"Victor is disrespectful," she said sharply, but her eyes were tender. "Your uncle is very busy—you know these things. Why you be fresh?"

"I'm sorry, Grandma," Victor dutifully apologized.

"Sometimes, I think it is wrong, the way your Mama baby you," she scolded. "Nothing to do with the business—always with school."

"Next year I graduate," he reminded her. "You want me to go into the business?" A challenge in his voice.

"You know what I feel, Victor." She was uncomfortable, talking this way in my presence. As though it was traitorous to her sons to concede that Victor might be happier on his own.

"Grandma, I'm a stinker," Victor said regretfully. "I know you want what's best for me." And best, for Victor, was away from family intrigue. All that money made little impression on Victor. I respected him for that.

"Is late," she said abruptly. I'd seen her anxious glances at Victor when he looked long at me. The Mazzini family wouldn't be happy if Victor showed serious interest in a skinny blonde. Not that there was going to be anything serious between us. "Let us go to our rooms. Victor, call Rosa for me. Then you can walk Andrea to her rooms."

I sat talking with Mama until Rosa appeared, to wheel her off. Then Victor and I went upstairs to the second floor, Victor lingering briefly in conversation at my door, before he sauntered down the corridor to his own rooms.

I opened the door, reached cautiously for the wall

switch. Welcoming the soft sweep of light that bathed my sitting room. Tony's exhortation echoed in my mind—"Lock the door when you're in your rooms." I turned to flip the lock into position, froze. My eyes galvanized to the sheet of white paper on the floor, I hadn't noticed it when I opened the door.

Trembling, guessing its message, I bent to pick up the plain white sheet, boldly inscribed—as before—in large, awkwardly printed block letters.

"TIME RUNNING OUT SIGNORINA. NEXT TIME YOU DIE."

CHAPTER

9

I stared at the white sheet, the letters taunting me, jumping up to smack me in the eyes. Carlo Mazzini wasn't here. To whom did I run this time? Not Victor, I cautioned myself uneasily. Victor would be shocked. He'd pack me up and ship me off to safety, on the first plane. Not Mama Mazzini, who was already concerned about me.

Mama hadn't said one word about the snake. But her eyes—at regular intervals this evening—had rested upon me with anxiety. No, I mustn't confront Mama with this ugly message.

I didn't want to leave the castle. I resented these threats. I wouldn't run away! No more than Dad had ever run away in the face of trouble. Stay here, I exhorted myself sternly. Stay here and—with Tony's help—ferret out who meant me harm. *Dig out the motive.*

I folded the white sheet of paper carefully into a small segment, as though by concealing the ominous words I was temporarily staving off the threat. To-morrow I must talk with Tony, I promised myself urgently. Tony was so very bright. He knew the villagers. From his grandfather he knew much of what happened in the castle, much about the domestic staff. Together, we'd find out who was behind these threats. With facts, I could go to Mama Mazzini—and she would quietly take action.

With the door locked behind me, I crossed from the sitting room to the door of the bedroom, reached with

one hand to grope into the darkness for the switch.
Painfully conscious of last night's confrontation when
I turned down the bed. And now this new warning
—"TIME RUNNING OUT SIGNORINA." *When* did
time run out?

Lamplight spilled about the bedroom. My eyes
cautiously inspected the room, fearful of what I might
find. From where would danger strike next? I believed that message. There would be another, more
ominous attempt. But no, *no,* I wasn't running away!
I was angry now. Furious, the way I'd seen Dad
furious when ugly threats were thrown at him. *He
never ran away.*

My eyes focused on the bed. I knew I must go
there, turn down the covers. Only then could I pretend to relax. Go on, Andrea. Turn down the covers!

There. No sinister visitor tonight, poised to spring
at me. Only gaily flowered sheets, unsullied by a
foreign presence. I kicked off my shoes, walked over
to the dresser, much too restless for sleep. But to
prepare for bed would be an activity.

I shivered faintly in the night coolness. Winter
pajamas tonight, I ordered myself. A summer vacation in the Alps had taught me to take along warm
clothing in the mountains. With audaciously red ski
pajamas in hand, I moved into the bathroom, remembering the electric panel in there that would provide
heat at the flip of a switch.

I lingered in the cozy warmth of the bathroom.
Relishing, for the moment, this small comfort. Delaying the moment when I must climb beneath the covers and flip off the lights.

In my red ski pajamas—red for courage, I jibed
myself—with paperback in hand, I hovered beside
the bed. Still reluctant to climb between the elegantly
silky sheets to settle down for the night. Determinedly, I strode away from the bed, settled myself in a
chair with a reading lamp adjacent.

I tried to concentrate on the novel before me. I
read the words automatically, comprehending little,

my mind assaulted by too many questions. To whom at the castle was I a threat? In what way? Oh, it was so absurd!

Not a threat to Mama Mazzini—my mind refused to consider this. The servants? Which one? Why? Nino? Nino remained the constantly suspicious figure— but was this because I found him personally repulsive?

Nino had left the castle early tonight, I forced myself to rationalize. While we were still at dinner. We'd heard the car pull out only a few minutes after he left the table. *It couldn't have been Nino.* No time for him to have gone up to my rooms, slipped the note under my door, and then gone out to the garage.

I abandoned the paperback, walked to a window to gaze out into the night. The sky lavishly sprinkled with stars, a great chunk of moon spreading light below. On impulse, I left the window, hurried to my closet to pull down a furry red robe with mandarin collar, covering me down to my toes.

Wrapped in the robe, I pulled open the windows that led to the small, wrought-iron wrapped balcony, stepped outside and lowered myself into the chaise. The air was cold, brisk. How exhilarating! Hardly what I needed to combat insomnia tonight, but it lent me a quasi peace.

I sniffed the heavy scent of the pines to the rear, the night scents of the roses, the honeysuckle, the carnations. Back in those woods a deer was calling. I smiled faintly, envisioning the deer by a stream. My eyes enjoyed the awesome sweep of mountains on all sides. I relished the night silence. But across my mind jogged the knowledge that somewhere below an armed man patrolled the grounds. Danger from without for some member of the Mazzini family—most likely, Mama. My danger lay within the castle walls.

I lay back in the chaise, my thoughts centering on Tony. Increasingly, questions about Tony tugged at me. I was certain Tony was keeping a wall between us. He knew much about the castle, about the Mazzinis, that he wasn't confiding to me. Did Tony know who threatened my life? What would he—could he—do about this?

I felt a recurrent guilt because I'd mentioned the hush-hush business merger the Mazzinis were planning with some cigarette company. It must be a merger of major magnitude. Any cigarette company, even the new, fledgling ones, represented multi-million dollar investments.

Could Tony be a plant for some rival firm? The possibility sent a zigzag of alarm through me. No, I was being melodramatic. Tony was Antonio's grandson!

Tony was far more cosmopolitan than the villagers because he'd lived away for years. At college, at work in New York. He had a keen mind. Naturally, he'd acquired a sophistication foreign to the villagers.

I started at the sound of footsteps below. At first, I thought it was the night patrol, which should have been reassuring but which turned me off because it heightened my awareness of danger about the castle. Then I heard voices.

"Aldo, bring the car out," Nino was ordering with his habitual arrogance. "Don't take all night."

"I'm glad you could come, Congressman," Nino's father was saying, his accent slight but unmistakably Sicilian. "Carlo expressed his regrets that he couldn't be here, but he's conferring with our Congressman friend in the midwest."

"The lobbying on something like this is bound to cost a fortune, Mr. Santini," the Congressman warned. "These people come high—and they must set up offices in Washington."

"Congressman, I've told you," Santini's voice rose, warmly complacent. "We'll pay all costs. Money is no consideration. Results are what counts."

"No guarantees, you know," the Congressman warned. "This is a tricky situation. We'll work like crazy to sell—but there's always the chance of an upset."

"Not when you're prepared to buy." Santini's voice carried a mild note of irritation. "It's a matter of timing, of paving the way. We've gone into this with every angle covered. Too much money is involved not to bring it off!"

The men were directly within my sight line now, with the moonlight spilling palely on their faces. They turned, at the sound of a car pulling out of the garage and rolling down the driveway.

Nino Santini's father—a smaller edition of his son, with the same arrogance about his once grossly handsome face, a thinness of the mouth that was unlike Nino's yet hinted at the same temperament. The other man, the Congressman, appeared vaguely familiar. I was sure I'd seen his face on TV newscasts, in the newspapers. I couldn't place a name with the face.

Nino reached to pull open the door for the two older men, who climbed into the rear. Nino slammed the door shut, slid into the front beside Aldo. The long, black Cadillac moved smoothly down the driveway.

Suddenly, I was cold. I didn't want to stay out here on the balcony. I hurried back into the bedroom, closed the windows. Locked them, though that was absurd. Who could climb up the balcony? Certainly not with the guard carrying a shotgun below.

In the morning, both Victor and Nino were at the breakfast table when I came downstairs. I'd expected Nino to be in the office by now. Sophia was bustling between breakfast room and kitchen, exchanging high-spirited raillery with Victor.

"Good morning!" Victor smiled brilliantly at me. Nino grunted.

"Good morning." My own smile—warm for Victor —slid across Nino to include Sophia, who was already pouring fragrant, strong coffee for me from the carafe on the table.

"Everything ready, Signorina," Sophia said complacently, her dark eyes moving wisely from Victor to me. "Sit. I bring." So Sophia suspected that Victor approved of my presence at the castle. *Would* he, if he knew?

I slid into a chair, reached for my coffee. I was uncomfortable beneath Nino's covert scrutiny. Like Sophia, he was conscious that I turned on Victor, and was annoyed. Mama, too, was uneasy about this. But Victor would be here only for a week or two. I'd never see him again. Didn't the others realize this?

Sophia was putting breakfast before me when Nino pushed back his chair, rose heavily to his feet.

"I have to go to work," he announced brusquely, his eyes brushing Victor and me with contempt. We were parasites. "I'm not the kinda guy that walks out on his responsibilities," he boasted. "The Don knows—he counts on me, and I'm there."

"Don't let us hold you up," Victor drawled.

My heart pounded as I watched the rage bubble up between them, threaten to spill over. But in a moment it was over. Nino shrugged, strode away, wary of tangling with the Don's favorite. Victor shot me a conspiratorial grin which plainly said that neither of us dug Nino Santini.

Victor and I sat talking companionably over Lucia's excellent breakfast, with Sophia waddling in regularly with extra sausages, hot rolls, a fresh carafe of coffee.

"Eat, eat," she exhorted, first Victor, then me.

Recurrently, my mind shot to Tony. I was ambivalent now about discussing this second note with him. Emotionally, I was eager to talk to him about everything that happened, to look to him for guidance. Yet my mind warned that I might be colossally naive. Tony might not be what he seemed. He could be involved in this cigarette company merger.

"Oh, I've been riding your bike," I reported to Victor, trying to push Tony from my mind. "It's great."

"Ride it every day," Victor encouraged. He pointed with mock disgust at his cast. "Good bike like that needs a workout," he jibed. "Your duty."

"It'll be a pleasure" I tossed back with a grin.

Giuseppe walked into the breakfast room. Automatically, I pushed back my chair.

"No rush, Signorina," he said quickly. "The Signora is in the small salon. Come when you have finished your breakfast. No rush," he repeated emphatically—and I was certain this was at Mama Mazzini's orders.

Still, I hurried through my second cup of coffee, went directly to the small salon. Victor had said he'd be right behind. He knew his great-grandmother relished every second of his company.

This morning, I'd been reading hardly half an hour before Mama waved the newspaper aside. Victor lifted his eyebrows in a humorous show of astonishment.

"Enough for this morning, Andrea," she said gently. "Take the bicycle, ride a while. I will sit here and fight with my great-grandson."

"Grandma, we never fight," Victor said with mock reproach.

"You stay and fight with me," she ordered, pretending to scowl. "You young ones—no respect for older people."

I left Mama and Victor alone, wondering if she were about to dress him down about a too overt interest in me. Mama was not one to be delicate when she was upset, I suspected. I heard them bickering affectionately as I sauntered from the room, knowing they were waiting for me to be out of earshot before Mama broached what was paramount on her mind.

I went out to the storeroom brought out the bike, walked with it to the pebbled path. Climbing onto the seat, I scanned the grounds for sight of Tony. This morning I was especially anxious to talk with him, because of the note, tucked away in the pocket of my tailored yellow silk blouse.

I moved slowly down the path, my heart thumping while my eyes searched for Tony. Nowhere in sight. Of course, he could be working at the other side of the castle. But I firmly squashed an impulse to ride around to the other side to search for him. No!

Thrown off-balance by Tony's absence, I headed unenthusiastically toward the walled-in avenue to the public road. I'd have to go through the bike-riding sequence, lest anyone watching should develop a suspicion that I was upset. Oh, I was being melodramatic again, I chided myself. How did I know Tony wasn't here? The grounds were enormous. He could be far beyond my sight now, show up later.

But quite suddenly, I knew this wasn't true. Because there, weeding a square of multi-colored carnations, was Antonio. Antonio was back! When would I see Tony again? *Would I see Tony again?*

"Hi there." Painfully casual, I smiled at Antonio. "It's good to see you back."

CHAPTER *But where was Tony?*

10 "*Grazie*, Signorina." He rose awkwardly into an upright position. "My arthritis—it come and go. Sometime, all right for a month . . ." He shrugged his incomprehension. "Maybe tomorrow, next day, start up again."

"I hope not." I managed the perfunctory response. But my heart pounded because Antonio's well-being meant Tony would not be here, when I so desperately wished to talk with him.

I smiled again, and pedaled slowly away. I felt the weight of Antonio's eyes, watching me. Had Tony talked to his grandfather about me? What was Antonio thinking?

Oh, why didn't I ask Antonio for his home phone? I could call Tony, talk to him. They had a phone—Tony had mentioned it that first morning, when he stood at the gates arguing with Rico. No! No, I can't phone—

I pedaled more swiftly, as though action would erase some of the tension that clamped about my shoulders. I was perched on top of a volcano, not knowing when it would explode. With no inkling of how to handle the situation, except that I was determined not to run.

I biked my usual distance, paused to rest. My black-eye-patched dog came over for a game of fetch. I dropped myself to a patch of lushly thick grass, with

121

the herd of black Angus behind the one line of
barbed wire across the road, and the mountains and
trees rising impressively on all sides. A study in pastoral calm—but within me a fermenting unease because, from out of nowhere, death could come wheeling down upon me.

I threw a stick. The dog gleefully pursued. I lay
back, using a tree trunk for a head rest. Throwing the
stick repeatedly, until the dog was panting from his
exertions.

"Sit," I ordered sternly.

He happily collapsed beside me. I reached out a
hand to scratch him behind the ears. Asking myself,
how do I reach Tony? Something within me balking
at phoning him, at making the first move. With all
this chemistry boiling over between us, he'd never
made a move to socialize.

I was watching the time closely. I had no desire to
return to the castle much before lunch. Sitting there,
I turned over in my mind everything I knew about
every single individual in the castle, without coming
up with any substantial clue as to who was trying to
drive me away—or, failing this, to kill. I'd suspected
Nino because I disliked him—and I knew he was
angry at my lack of response to his advances. But
logic forced me to concede that Nino could not have
been responsible for last night's note. I could pin this
down on no one.

Suddenly restless, needing movement, I rose to my
feet, tossed the stick for one last time today for my
canine friend, and climbed aboard the bike, my mind
running a montage of the increasingly ominous
threats beamed at me. Tony hadn't brushed them
aside. He'd said, "Lock your door." What did Tony
know that I didn't?

Back at the castle, I put the bicycle away in the
storeroom, walked down the corridor toward the
staircase.

"Andrea," Victor was calling to me from the sitting
room off the terrace.

"Hi."

Victor and Mama were sitting by the open casement windows.

"Don't you feel smug?" Victor jeered humorously. "All that healthy exercise this morning?"

"It was beautiful." I smiled at Mama, noticing how she was lacing and unlacing her surprisingly small, heavily veined hands. Something about the conference with Victor had not been satisfying. She was disturbed.

"Lucia will be ready with lunch shortly," Mama said, trying not to display her distress.

"Great, I'm starving." I managed a show of enthusiasm. Mama enjoyed the presence of a hearty appetite.

How lovely if we could lunch out on the terrace, I thought wistfully, gazing at the gracious area off the sitting room provided with table and chairs. But on the terrace, Mama Mazzini would be a target for one of those "enemies" that she'd spoken about. Business people over whom Carlo Mazzini evidently trampled on his road to the top—and now he feared for his mother's life. There must have been threats! As there were threats now against my life. But what possible connection could there be between Mama Mazzini and me? None, that I could pin down.

"You eat like a bird," Mama chided with mock severity. "Never please Lucia that way."

"I'll do better," I promised soothingly. "Right now I'd better run upstairs and wash up."

By the time I'd come downstairs again, Victor was wheeling Mama into the dining room. Nino was already at the table, his chair shoved back to allow him to cross his legs while he alternately swigged from a glass in his hands and studied the stock market page of the *New York Times*, which I gathered Aldo picked up for him daily from a nearby resort town where they stocked city newspapers. At Mama's arrival, he reluctantly relinquished his newspaper and grunted a greeting.

Nino ate with his usual voracious appetite and bad table manners, speaking little through luncheon. Neither Victor nor Mama appeared to notice his ill-tempered silence. They must be accustomed to this.

"Andrea, what about a drive about the countryside after lunch?" Victor invited. "After all, you can't get far on a bike!"

"I'd like that," I accepted with warmth. But I saw the way Nino stopped eating, to stare with contempt at Victor for extending this invitation. "That is, if—" I turned to Mama Mazzini. We'd developed a pattern of reading after breakfast and after dinner, but Mama had every right to switch this around.

"Go, Andrea," Mama said firmly. "We read after dinner. Makes a nice evening for me. With television I fall asleep." She turned to Victor. "Give Aldo time to have his lunch first," she warned.

I realized why Mama Mazzini was not perturbed at the prospect of Victor and me spending an afternoon together. With the cast on his foot, Victor wasn't driving. Aldo would be sitting up front all the time.

What did Mama think about the snake incident, I asked myself again? She had not made one comment. I knew she must be upset. And now there was the second note to worry about. But Mama didn't know even about the first . . .

Nino left the table the instant he had finished his lunch, with a mumbled, *"Scusi, Zia."* Victor went off to alert Aldo to the afternoon assignment while Mama and I lingered over coffee. I was trying desperately to hold on to my cool, because I *was* upset. No matter how I mentally rebelled about being pushed around, logic told me to pack up and cut out of the castle. But logic couldn't move from the starting gate when I felt so turned on for Tony.

Victor, walking with remarkable ease considering the cast, came into the dining room to say that Aldo had brought the car out front. Simultaneously, Giuseppe appeared to wheel Mama to the elevator.

"There's an animal farm quite near," Victor recalled, his eyes gently teasing me. "Are you too so-phisticated for such juvenile shenanigans?"

"I'd love it," I said promptly. Walking about an animal farm, we wouldn't have Aldo listening in to every word we said and probably reporting to Nino. "I'm mad for almost everything four-legged."

"I used to go to this place the first summers we came to the castle," Victor said reminiscently. "The big scene was to feed the deer."

We strolled from the castle, out to the waiting car. A small, inconspicuously black Volvo this time. I sus-pected Victor had deliberately picked this one out. I couldn't imagine him preferring one of the Cadillac limousines which sat in the garage, or the flamboyant-ly red Mercedes Benz.

Victor talked about the week at Fire Island, when he'd broken the metatarsal bone in his foot, about revolt at his college, staying with the impersonal ap-proach, however, always conscious of Aldo's presence at the wheel. And, I suspected, chafing at that presence. We were both glad when we pulled up before a long, low, fieldstone-trimmed building, which was luncheonette, gift shop, and entrance to the animal farm.

"The last time I was at a zoo," I recalled, walking beside Victor into the building, "it was my eleventh birthday. We were leaving in a few days for Sicily. Dad took me to lunch at Schrafft's, and then to Cen-tral Park Zoo."

"You love your father very much," Victor said, his voice oddly pensive. "You respect him."

"Yes—" The truth about my parents hovered on the tip of my tongue, but loyalty to Dean Benedict held me silent.

"I love my father," Victor conceded. "I don't under-stand him. I never will. I don't understand my grand-father."

"The much-publicized generation gap?" I flipped. But the anguish in Victor's eyes touched me.

"For us, it's more than that. We live in different

cultures. My grandfather, my father, despite all the years here in America, are steeped in the old Sicilian ways. My father was *born* here, but—" He gestured unhappily. "I don't dig their scene."

Victor reached into his pocket for bills. A teenager, at the cash register, obviously admiring Victor, gave us souvenir literature and pointed us to the door. We walked out into the sprawling acreage, neatly arranged to show off the animals. The paths edged with white-washed stones, masses of petunias everywhere. Off to one side, a pond, the domain of ducks and swans.

We stopped off to laugh at the antics of the monkeys, fed them nuts bought from a coin machine. Marveled at the majesty of a mountain lion prowling a huge rock enclosed by a storm fence.

"How do you like the deer?" Victor prodded me along a side path. Behind fences deer of various ages sat or pranced with unbelievable grace. Fawns came eagerly to nuzzle at the fence, for the corn they knew we couldn't resist buying to feed them.

We lingered with the deer, enchanted by their friendliness, at last moved off to an open area where sheep and goats, a peacock with a belligerent crow at his heels, a mother llama and a young one at her heels roamed among the zoo visitors.

"Mama's brazen enough," Victor said with relish, while the mother llama ate from his hand, and long-legged baby nuzzled shyly at its mother's side.

We walked for what seemed to be acres, enjoying the casual, relaxed atmosphere. And then Victor took my arm and led me to another side path.

"The reptile pit is just ahead," he began.

"No!" I said quickly, suddenly trembling. "I—I'm terrified of snakes."

"Most are harmless, you know," he chided gently.

"I'd rather not see them, Victor." I fought to hold on to my cool. All at once I was starkly conscious of the danger that lay waiting for me at the castle. I saw that red, white and black banded snake in my bed—

and it *could* have been a rattler. I was at the mercy of someone unknown to me. I walked in the shadows of death. The note said this so clearly. "TIME RUNNING OUT SIGNORINA. NEXT TIME YOU DIE." I struggled for a smile. "Shall we go, Vic?"

We left the animal farm, lingered briefly in a booth in the luncheonette section, gorging on fantastic sundaes. From where we sat we could see Aldo, sprawled on the front seat of the Volvo, drinking a can of soda while he read the *New York News*, which he'd picked up in the gift shop.

"I have to fly down to New York day after tomorrow," Victor reported. "To have the foot checked out. But I'll be back the next day."

"I'm glad you're coming back," I said impulsively, and felt my face grow hot because Victor was gazing at me with quiet pleasure at this reaction. But I hadn't meant it the way he was interpreting my outburst.

We left the luncheonette, settled ourselves in the back seat of the Volvo. Victor talked to me, was warm, attentive, yet now I felt that his mind was far away. Victor was grappling with serious problems—his father, I guessed with compassion.

"Shall we drive around for a while?" Victor offered. "There's some unbelievable views about two miles to the east."

"Perhaps we ought to head back," I suggested. Instinct told me he would be relieved. There, he *was*. "I am supposed to be on duty," I reminded with a chuckle.

"To Grandma you're a guest," Victor insisted, but he leaned forward to tell Aldo, "Back to the castle, please."

The conversation on our return drive was necessarily restricted by Aldo's presence behind the wheel. But it had been a pleasant side trip. I was glad we'd come.

"Oh, I know a couple of really jazzy landmarks

around here," Victor recalled, as we pulled up at the
gates. "Why don't we give them a whirl?"

"Fine." I smiled effervescently, yet inwardly I was
uneasy. To me this was a delightful summer friendship, with no romantic intent. I knew Victor was
pursuing a more serious course. It shone from his
eyes. I was reluctant to see him hurt. I might not be
in love with Vic—but he was special.

In the castle, we both went up to our rooms, I with
a certain disinclination. My elegant rooms wore over-
tones of foreboding now. Every time I crossed the
threshold my throat tightened, my pulse quickened.

Inside the sitting room, I remembered Tony's exhortation. I locked the door. Even though I had no
intention of remaining here until dinner. Tony. When
was I going to see him again? How could I contrive
this?

Restless indoors, I went out on the small balcony of
my sitting room. I dropped onto the chaise, picked up
a magazine lying on the floor. What was that? A car
coming up the road? I leaned forward. A vintage
car, immaculately maintained. It was pulling to a
stop below.

Father Marchesi stepped out of the car, slammed
the door shut, walked toward the entrance. Fleetingly, I was alarmed. Had something happened to Mama
Mazzini?

I darted inside, across to the door, cracked it. I
could hear Rosa talking with Father Marchesi. Calmly, about the weather. No, nothing was wrong. I was
relieved. There, Mama Mazzini was being wheeled
down the corridor to greet Father Marchesi. Mama
was unable to travel to Father Marchesi's church, so
Father Marchesi came to Mama.

I didn't want to stay upstairs. Why should I, on
such a glorious day? Go downstairs, walk about the
grounds. In the back of my mind—though I refused
to acknowledge it—was the hope that I'd fall into
conversation with Antonio, that he'd talk about Tony.
I was still pursued by the need to talk to Tony about

this second warning, even while I knew I was being unrealistic. *What could Tony do?*

I walked out into the late afternoon sunlight, took the path to the left, past the wing that held both the chapel and the offices. I walked slowly, inspecting the lavish display of the rose bushes. Heard the slow intonation of Father Marchesi's voice, in Latin. Moved hurriedly away, feeling myself an intruder.

I walked about the expanse of grounds without once seeing Antonio. Then, retracing my steps, I caught a glimpse of him, walking down the path to the walled avenue. I'd forgotten about the five o'clock curfew for the day help. Antonio was hurrying, despite his arthritis, to avoid Rico's phoning up to the castle to check on his whereabouts.

Disappointed, I took a shortcut across the left wing of the castle. Time to go upstairs and change for dinner. Passing, again, the heavily flowered rose bushes that fronted the left wing, I paused, leaned forward to inhale their fragrance. Unaware that this was just beneath Nino's window until his voice filtered out to me. He was talking with someone on the phone.

"Look, don't worry," Nino was insisting expansively. "We got fifty-five thousand acres sewed up in the Islands. My uncle, Mr. Mazzini, has the deeds—he's coming with them to the castle. We got options on another fifty thousand acres. Whenever the thing goes through, we roll into action!"

I straightened up, disconcerted by Nino's voice, so close—and stared directly into his eyes for one unnerving moment.

"Wait," he said harshly into the phone. "I'll be right with you."

Nino leaned forward, drew the casement windows tight, his face ugly with rage. My heart pounding, I moved hurriedly away.

So Carlo Mazzini was coming to the castle. I'd go to him immediately with this second note. He'd have to concede he'd been wrong about the mentally

retarded relative. If he didn't already know who was
to blame, he could find out. A man with his fantastic
power would know what to do.

He'd have to stop playing games with my life. I
doubted that Carlo Mazzini would want a murder on
his hands!

After dinner I read to Mama Mazzini in the small
salon. Nino and Victor were watching baseball on
TV, in the sitting room off the terrace. Tonight Mama
was tired. More from the tensions in the castle, I
suspected, than from physical weariness. I knew she
was upset about her private conference with Victor.
Did it concern me?

Victor appeared in the doorway, grinned affectionately at his great-grandmother, whose chin was
again descending to her chest.

"I'll send in Giuseppe," he said, and disappeared
down the corridor.

Moments later Giuseppe came into the room, firmly
insisted—despite her protests—that Mama go up to
bed. I neatly folded the half-read newspaper, placed
it on the desk for the next session with Mama.

Alone, I sat restlessly pretending to be avidly interested in the copy of *Life* which Victor had left here
earlier. My mind refused to settle on the magazine.
Where was Vic? If he were here this minute I'd
tell him about everything. Though instinct warned
against this. Victor would permit no gambles with
my life.

I crossed to the window, looked out into the night.
Was Victor out walking about the grounds? He did
that sometimes at night, I knew, despite the cast on
his foot. Mama had chided him about the solitary
night walking. The mountain air was dangerous at
night, she claimed, leaning on some ancient supersti-
tion, I supposed.

I became aware of a heavy thirst as I stubbornly
forced myself to flip through the magazine. Lucia's
highly spiced shrimp with mushrooms and wine, I

suspected, and decided to go out to the kitchen to ask for a tall glass of chilled fruit juice.

The kitchen was well-lighted, but Lucia had, evidently, gone off duty for the night. The kitchen wore that end-of-the-day appearance. Nobody would mind, I jibed at myself humorously, if I went into the refrigerator and helped myself to a glass of fruit juice.

I looked into the refrigerator, found a frosted carafe of orange juice that, in view of my thirst, was intensely inviting. I poured a tall glass to the top, returned the carafe to the refrigerator, and walked to the window, sipping greedily.

A fog sat heavily over the grounds, blotting out the impressive view of the mountains. A treacherous night for driving—it would be impossible to see the side of the road. Would Carlo Mazzini be coming to the castle tonight? Nino said his uncle was "coming to the castle"—he hadn't mentioned a specific time. Oh, let him come up tonight! At the very first chance, I'd talk to him.

"Well, look who's here!" Nino's voice was triumphant, mocking. I spun about in shock. "Drinking all by yourself in the kitchen? That's not very friendly." He was swaggering toward me, grinning broadly.

"Orange juice," I said, panic tightening my throat.

"Sure it's not spiked with vodka?" he jibed, moving so closely I flinched before his wine-heavy breath. "Here, let me see."

Nino took the glass from me, managing to pin me against the wall while he tasted the orange juice. Why had I come out here this way? This was exactly the kind of situation I'd been avoiding since I laid eyes on Nino Santini.

"What do you know?" He chortled. "Orange juice." He leaned over to deposit the glass on the windowsill, keeping me imprisoned by the length of his massive arm. "A gorgeous chick like you ought to be having a ball in some classy ginmill."

"Let me by, please," I said, as coolly as I could

manage. My heart was pounding at his repulsive closeness.

"What's the rush, Miss Nosey? Thought you were getting yourself an earful out there, didn't you?" My face colored guiltily. "Don't do that, baby. People don't try that around here—" His hands moved in, to fondle my shoulders. I stiffened in rejection.

"Let me go!" My eyes blazed while I shrank from the touch of his huge, perspiring hands. He laughed, gloating because I couldn't physically escape him. "Let me go!" My voice soared shrilly. He laughed again. My hand swung out to slap him resoundingly across one cheek. At the identical moment, I became aware of Victor, striding toward us.

"Let her go, Nino," Victor ordered with quiet intensity. "*Step aside.*"

Nino's face stained an ugly red. He glared furiously at Victor, then at me. He muttered something under his breath while he released me, then stalked from the room. I trembled. Oh, I had made myself a formidable enemy this time! Hadn't the situation been ugly enough before? Why must I make an enemy of Nino Santini?

"Andrea, I'm sorry," Victor apologized quietly. "Nino can be an awful boor."

"He's furious with me," I said uneasily, even while I was relieved that he was gone.

"Don't worry about Nino," Victor soothed. "Nino makes a lot of noise, but he won't bother you again. My grandfather won't tolerate that kind of behavior in the castle. And Nino knows I'll report it if he starts up again."

Still, I remembered the rage in Nino's eyes, and shivered. I'd slapped him—and Victor saw. Nino's ego was badly damaged. I thought about the one time I'd been taken to a bullfight—only because I'd insisted on going. I was in Madrid with Dad, where he was covering a story, and a bullfight had seemed so romantic. The bull, plunging toward the matador, reminded me of Nino. I'd shivered then, for the matador.

"I was thirsty," I picked up self-consciously. "I came out here for something to drink."

"We're all thirsty tonight." Unexpectedly, Victor chuckled. "Lucia's shrimps. That seasoning!" He whistled expressively. His eyes settled on the half-filled glass of orange juice I was picking up from the windowsill. "I believe I'll have myself some of that. It looks good."

"I'll get it for you." I was disconcerted by the intensity of his gaze. Oh, please, Victor, don't make romantic overtures. "Why don't you sit down?" He

133

managed well with the cast on his foot, but I knew it was tiring.

"Such service," he ribbed gently.

Victor wasn't going to make a pitch, though his eyes said much. I should have understood that Victor was far too sensitive to try a romantic approach after what had just happened with Nino. If I didn't feel the way I did about Tony, I could easily persuade myself that I could fall in love with Victor. Wow, wouldn't that set the Mazzini family on its ear! Victor was expected to marry a rich young Sicilian, to satisfy his grandfather. Sicilian at least by descent.

I poured a tall glass of orange juice for Victor, carried it to him, sat down beside him at Lucia's kitchen table. How quiet here, with the domestic staff off to their rooms. I was aware of a rare kind of peace. Like the stillness before a hurricane strikes, my mind carelessly chose an image. And fear wrapped itself about me again.

Victor, sensing that I was uptight, talked about a trip to Aruba during his last Christmas vacation at school.

"I've never seen water like that," he said with quiet pleasure. "Blue-green, unbelievably beautiful. At night, it was enough just to sit on my balcony and gaze out there at the water, endlessly—or walk along the beach with this pooch who kind of adopted my roommate and me. I'd like to go back there again." He laughed reminiscently. "I've never looked at water so long, so intensely, in all my life."

"I love the ocean," I said. Remembering the seaports of Sicily. Remembering Fire Island in early November, when the summer people were all gone. "Even Jones Beach in winter," I admitted, laughing faintly.

Victor and I had so much in common. The realization was, somehow, reassuring. As long as Victor remained at the castle, I felt immeasurably safer.

We finished our orange juice, taking longer than necessary. Then Victor walked me upstairs to my rooms. A heavy, night quiet pervading the atmosphere. But while Victor lingered briefly in conversation at my door, we heard a car charge down the driveway, at far too high a speed. We both knew it was Nino, racing off to drink away his rage.

"Sleep well, Andrea," Victor said softly, and left me to go to his own rooms, far down the corridor.

Inside my sitting room, I carefully locked the door, left a lamp on until the bedroom was lighted, always conscious of danger. But what could happen to me here within my rooms, with the door locked and an armed sentry parading the grounds below?

The Mazzini family guarded against danger from the outside, my mind nastily insisted on emphasizing. Danger, for me, existed within the castle. My throat went dry as I remembered Nino's rage when I slapped him. A rage that was blown up a hundredfold because Victor witnessed this humiliation.

Nino's kind of animal fury was unnerving. Even while logic forced me to exempt him from that last threat—the second note thrust under my door—I knew that his current rage presented fresh danger. I had no way of knowing to what lengths Nino would go to salvage his ego.

I dawdled about getting to bed, because I dreaded the moment when I must switch off the lamps, entrust myself to darkness. Fleetingly, I toyed with the prospect of leaving one lamp lit all night. No, I couldn't, logic rejected. The sentry might notice, be concerned that something was wrong. I shuddered before the prospect of someone banging on my door in the middle of the night, when I was fast asleep, to inquire about a light burning in my rooms.

I read in bed for a while, clutching at a reason for keeping a light on. But my eyes were drooping sleepily. How ridiculous, to doze over a book! Resolutely, I put aside my novel, reached over to switch off the lamp. With blackness whirling in about me, I settled back against the pillows, fully expecting to fall asleep in an instant.

In the darkness, I was suddenly wide awake. The intermittent dozing had taken the edge off sleep for me. Still, I'd fall asleep in a few minutes, I promised myself, shifting about to the most comfortable position.

I tried one position, then another. Tossing restlessly. Straining to hear—and identify—every faint sound. Oh, this was absurd! I tossed back the covers, crossed to the windows. Feeling guilty at this childlike subterfuge, I pulled the drapes apart slightly, which allowed wedges of moonlight to spill into the room. There, I was no longer in complete blackness. With some minor comfort, I crawled back beneath the covers.

My sleep was broken, beset by troubled dreams. With the intrusion of morning sunlight, I came fully awake. Knowing I wouldn't sleep again. I lifted myself on one elbow, squinted at the clock on my bedside table. Just past six. This would be a long day, I warned myself ruefully.

I lay back against the pillows again. Not yet ready to face the day. All right, stay in bed another hour, I ordered myself. Try to relax. In an hour, I'd get up, dress, go downstairs for coffee. I'd take out Victor's bicycle, go riding about the countryside. It would clear my head, to put distance between the castle and myself for a while.

I switched over onto my tummy, burrowed my face in the pillow, hardly refreshed from the few hours of restless sleep. When I was uptight this way, I needed more than normal sleep. Now, lying here in the stillness of my bedroom, last night's incident in the kitchen raced thunderously, repetitively, through my mind. Why didn't Nino leave? His wife was pregnant—why didn't he go home to her?

Could I stop and talk casually with Antonio, ask about Tony? My heart thumped as I considered this. My mind framed casual sentences. *I must find some way to see Tony.*

I stalled—as I'd promised myself—until seven.

Then I arose, showered, dressed, went downstairs. No sounds anywhere in the castle. I walked down the corridor, turned off to the kitchen. I could see Lucia outside, leaning over her cherished herb garden, carefully choosing what she would need for the day's meals. She was too absorbed to notice me.

Coffee, deep amber now, was perking on the range. I brought down an earthenware mug of the kind that Lucia herself used, and poured myself fragrant, strong coffee, took it to the breakfast room. I pushed aside a generous segment of the butter-yellow café curtains to allow the sunlight to dart across the walnut table top.

How different the kitchen seemed this morning, I thought whimsically, while Lucia returned to the kitchen with the herbs cradled in both hands. She spied me, put the herbs into a bowl, and hurried toward me.

"How come you no sleep, Signorina?" she rebuked. "Is summer—you sleep."

"Not this morning," I laughed. "I got ahead on my sleep."

"Wait," Lucia ordered. "I bring you *torcetti*. Should be ready now."

Lucia went to the bank of gleaming wall ovens, pulled a pan of golden crescents, faintly brushed with powdered sugar, from the top oven. With amazing delicacy, she reached with one thick, squat hand to pile a plate high, and brought it to me.

"Oh, Lucia, I'll never be able to go back to school in my own clothes," I protested. But I was already lifting a flaky crescent to my mouth. No dessert for dinner, though.

I ate more than I intended, allowed Lucia to press a second large mug of coffee upon me. All the while, I was scanning the scenery. And then my eyes settled on Antonio. My pulse was hammering away.

Yes, I'll talk to Antonio. I'll just happen to pedal past him on the bike. I'll ask about Tony—that's natural enough, isn't it? Maybe he'll say something . . .

Self-conscious with intrigue, I left the breakfast

room, went to the storeroom to bring out the bicycle.
The castle still caught up in early morning quiet. I
heard Giuseppe talking to Rosa out in the corridor.
But nobody would notice that I stopped to chat with
Antonio. What if they did notice? It was mere
courtesy to stop to inquire about his health, after all
the days he'd been absent.

Antonio was weeding the carnations. He glanced
up, nodded with his usual friendliness as I approached,
halted beside him.

"The carnations will be opening soon, won't they?"
I asked with a show of avid interest.

"Sì, Signorina." He nodded with proprietary pride.
"One more week, maybe ten days. While I was sick
with the arthritis, I make sure Tony feed them right.
Is important, even this late." It seemed to me that he
looked about to see if we were observed. My heart
suddenly pounded. "Tony a good boy most of the
time. But right now—" He shook his head, chuckled.
"When he should be in fields, he go out with motorbike. Love that thing," Antonio said with mock disgust. "Out on the road right now, when he belong
working in the field. This road—" He pointed below,
then gestured toward the farmhouse past which I
usually rode. "Not much cars come."

"That's why I like to bike there," I said, exhilarated
by Antonio's information. The glint in his eyes told
me he was as intent on relaying this information as I
had been on obtaining it. It was a message from
Tony! I smiled gratefully, pedaled away.

I pedaled in the direction of the old farm, as Antonio had directed, straining for sight of Tony. The
road ahead seemed empty—of cars or motorbikes.
Had Tony become impatient, left?

I pedaled on determinedly, close to a mile, this
morning ignoring my four-legged friend who rushed
forward eagerly. I waved and continued to pedal. He
trotted along beside me for a short distance, then
philosophically abandoned his attempts at renewing
our friendship.

I squinted in the early morning sunlight, almost giving up hope of encountering Tony. I slowed down, debating about going ahead. Then I stiffened expectantly. Oh, yes, there he was! Right ahead, at the side of the road. The motorbike parked. Tony leaning against a tree, reading a newspaper.

Tony glanced up, saw me, waved. He folded the newspaper, and tucked it into a back pocket.

"I'm goofing off from work," he reported leisurely as I approached. "I should have been in the field by six." And I knew—I saw the smugness in his eyes— that his grandfather and he had plotted to arrange this little rendezvous this morning.

"No day for the fields," I protested, for the moment effervescent.

"How are things at the castle?" he asked casually. But his eyes were serious.

Instantly, my effervescence evaporated.

"New developments," I admitted somberly. "Another note stuck under my door." I dug into my slacks pocket to pull forth the single sheet of paper. "Here—"

He read, his face grim.

"I don't dig this," he said, frowning. "I can't see what kind of threat you present to anybody in the castle. Not to the Mazzini family. Not to the servants—" He squinted, rereading the note. "There's Nino, of course—"

"It couldn't have been Nino," I admitted.

Tony looked at me sharply.

"Why not?"

I explained that the time element completely vindicated Nino. And instinct told me Nino wouldn't resort to anything like a note. Nino would act.

"Not that Nino's been the little Boy Scout," I added, tensing with recall. "We had an ugly little scene in the kitchen last night." Tersely I briefed him.

Tony's eyes smoldered with anger. His jaw tightened pugnaciously.

"Nino Santini is a bad egg. Give him as wide a berth as you can."

"I intend to." I tried to laugh.

"I ought to make you pack up, cut out of the castle today," Tony said uneasily. "Too much is piling up that we can't figure out—"

"I have nowhere to go, actually," I objected quickly. "Except a furnished room back near the campus." I took a deep breath, pulled out Dean Benedict's lie, which made me so uncomfortable. "My parents are in Europe." I could have arranged earlier, I told him, to have stayed at Suzy's apartment in New York. But now Suzy was tearing around Europe, and her parents were down at St. Croix for the summer.

"Andrea—" Tony gazed earnestly at me, reached for my hands. "I don't want you to leave!" He seemed indecisive, though. "I know you ought to run, fast—"

And, with one fluid movement, I was in Tony's arms. His mouth on mine. His arms holding me closely. Promising me so much. Safe this way, with Tony. Oh, I could stay this way forever!

"Andrea—" His face was against mine. "Andrea, I didn't mean for it to happen this way. So quickly—"

"What does it matter?" I challenged. Why did he sound unhappy? What did time matter? No doubts in my mind any more. Tony was in love with me. "Two weeks or two months, what's the difference?" Why did he seem so upset? "Tony, what's wrong about us?"

"Baby, it's great." He smiled tenderly. "Only, I feel rotten about your staying at the castle—"

"I have to stay, Tony," I insisted impulsively. To be close to him. "I'm staying," I reiterated firmly. Tony seemed ambivalent—glad and anxious, simultaneously. "Darling, don't worry—I'll be careful. Nothing can happen to me in broad daylight. In the evening—in the castle—I'll make a point of staying close to Mama Mazzini. Nobody'll dare try anything when I'm with her. I'll lock my door—I've been doing that since you told me, Tony—" I was running out of breath in my anxiety to reassure him.

"Lock the windows that open onto balconies, also," Tony ordered. "Don't go out on the balconies, even in daylight. They're hazardous areas. Never leave the castle once the sun sets, Andrea."

"I won't," I promised, rashly brushing aside alarm because something new—beautiful—filled my mind. The image of Tony and me together, for the rest of our lives. Tony was cautious. He was determined not to rush. For my sake, I thought tenderly. "Tony, I'll be careful. And as soon as Mr. Mazzini arrives, I'll go to him with the note. He'll do something, Tony. You'll see."

"Mazzini is scheduled to come up soon?" Tony's eyes were quizzical.

"I don't know when," I acknowledged. "I gather it'll be any day." Again, guilt brushed me. Everything about the Mazzini-engineered merger was supposed to be top secret. Yet here I was, spilling information as casually as though I were discussing the weather. But Tony had a right to know, I coddled my sense of guilt. Carlo Mazzini's arrival at the castle concerned my life.

"Andrea, if you can, find out when he's due," Tony said carefully. I stared at him in shock. "I'd like to know, honey. Don't call me from the castle. I'll come back here tomorrow morning." And then explained, "With Carlo Mazzini here, I feel you're in less danger. This is his kingdom," Tony reminded, with a whimsical smile.

"All right, Tony," I promised.

My heart pounded. Tony was lying to me. He had another, covert reason for wanting to know when Carlo arrived at the castle. *Tony wasn't what he pretended to be.* He was here to spy on Carlo Mazzini. On the Mazzini family.

I remembered what Mama had said about the enemies of the family—the murdered son, Carlo's brother—and I felt sick inside. Oh, Tony couldn't be mixed up in anything evil. I refused to believe that! Business, yes. Something to do with the merger. But Tony could never be involved in murder.

Still, I was upset. I knew Tony was not what he seemed. What about the romantic interest in me? All part of a calculated plan? *Was Tony using me?*

I went back to the castle with my mind in chaos. Was I wrong in passing on what must obviously be top-secret information? What was Tony's part in this Mazzini family intrigue? Was he working for a rival cigarette company? Or was Tony involved in the real estate transaction? Fifty-five thousand acres already tied up, another fifty thousand in negotiation—that could be a fantastic commission. *What was Tony keeping from me?*

I put away the bicycle in the storeroom, went inside to breakfast, steeling myself to coming face to face with Nino. He wasn't there. Victor was at the table alone, reading the *New York Times*. He glanced up at my approach, smiled.

"I'm driving down to New York ahead of schedule," he reported with a sigh. "Driving—not flying," he emphasized philosophically. "That is, Aldo is driving me."

"Why driving?" I asked curiously. It was such a quick haul by plane. Already regretting Victor's absence. It was comforting to be with Victor.

"This rotten cast," Victor complained. "The heel popped off. I can't maneuver very well without it—no leverage. Oh, I'll be able to hop around here, but I'd never make it to New York by plane. We'll be leaving after breakfast. I was scheduled to go in to the doctor tomorrow anyway, so I suppose I shouldn't be so teed off."

"You'll be coming right back?" I tried for a casual note.

"Tomorrow." Victor's eyes were asking questions. I

could feel myself coloring. Why did I keep asking
questions that gave Victor the wrong impression?

While Victor and I were eating, we heard a car
rolling out of the garage. I leaned forward, to see the
Cadillac with Aldo at the wheel, cutting around to
the front of the castle.

"Rosa," Victor called into the kitchen. "Will you
please tell Aldo I'll be out in about ten minutes? I'm
having another cup of coffee."

"Si, Signor Victor," Rosa trilled, and waddled out
of the kitchen, down the corridor to the front entrance to the castle.

"Andrea, don't worry about Nino," Victor urged
quietly. "He can't cause you any trouble."

"I know," I said. Not knowing at all.

Victor left. I felt frighteningly alone. I lingered
uneasily over another cup of coffee because this kept
me close to the kitchen, where Lucia and Rosa chat-
tered away companionably. When Mama Mazzini
sent Giuseppe to tell me she was waiting in the small
salon, I ran eagerly to join her.

This morning we read at great length, though I
sensed that Mama was preoccupied. There was a look
about her that reminded me of Rembrandt's old
ladies. Compassion blending with resignation in her
eyes. A fine old lady trying to cope—and discovering
this most difficult.

Mama and I lunched alone. We'd heard a car pull
out of the garage earlier, and I'd suspected this was
Nino. Driving himself this morning because Victor
had taken off with Aldo. I would be spared seeing
him for another few hours, I thought with gratitude.

After lunch, when Mama was wheeled off to her
rooms for her afternoon rest, I decided, also, to try for
a nap. I was tired, heavy-eyed, from the lack of sleep
last night. Behind the locked door, I decided to make
a production of my aloneness. I soaked in a warm,
perfumed tub, feeling—on the surface—amazingly
sybaritic. Out of the tub, I slid into summer pajamas,

went out to the bed, carefully folded back the elegant red-and-plum cut-velvet spread, the light blankets.

The firm mattress beneath my back, at this hour of the day, seemed the ultimate in luxury. I closed my eyes, commanded myself to relax. More quickly than I'd anticipated, sleep overtook me.

I awoke with a start, taking a few moments to reorient myself. Lying quite still beneath the sheet, listening to the sounds below. A car crunched over the pebbled driveway, coming to a squeaky stop.

I tossed back the sheet. In bare feet, I hurried curiously into the sitting room, from which windows I had a view of the driveway below. Perhaps Carlo Mazzini was arriving. Oh, I hoped so!

I peered avidly out the window, watching the men emerging from the black Cadillac limousine, which Nino had been driving. Three men, in addition to Nino. None of them Carlo Mazzini. I sighed in disappointment.

Knowing I was unobserved, I inspected the men as closely as the distance permitted. None of them appeared to be Wall Street types, despite what I suspected was expensive tailoring. But Carlo Mazzini would hardly have assigned Nino to conduct business with Wall Street operators.

Tony was anxious to know when Carlo was arriving. But I wasn't to phone him from the castle, I recalled—he'd made a point of saying he'd be there in the morning. Tony's voice ricocheted in my mind now—"If you can, find out when he's due."

Why did Tony want to know? That question rode repetitiously through my mind. Was I a means to an end to Tony? Was I so infatuated with Tony that I couldn't see clearly? No! No, I won't think that way!

I went back into the bedroom, forced myself to concentrate on dressing for dinner. The last time there were male guests, Mama and I had dinner together in her rooms. Except for the occasion with Father Marchesi, of course. What about tonight? I didn't particularly look forward to dinner with Nino

and his guests. But even while I was thinking about
this, I heard the knock on my door.

I reached quickly for the zipper at the back of my
would-be Pucci print, hurried to the door.

"Yes?" My hand on the door, but not yet opening it.
Conscious that death could stalk behind any door.

"Giuseppe, Signorina," he said, and I quickly pulled
the door wide. "The Signora wishes you to have dinner with her in her rooms. Any time you are ready."

"Thank you, Giuseppe. I'll only be five minutes."

I brushed my hair, told myself that by having dinner with Mama, I was avoiding another encounter
with Nino. The guests, of course, were here on business. In the Mazzini family, women had no part in
such matters.

Mama seemed faintly apologetic about our dining
together in her sitting room, for the second time in
the short while that I had been at the castle.

"Nino have business people here, Andrea," Mama
explained, her smile conciliatory. "Better we eat up
here, not bother with that business talk. Let them be
alone. Money," she scoffed. "All they talk about is
making money."

After dinner I read as usual, Mama making me stop
to reread passages at frequent intervals, as though
her mind was not thoroughly involved and she was
being conscientious about absorbing every minute de-
tail that revolved about names familiar to her.

"You're tired," I said gently, when we'd covered the
items of usual interest to Mama Mazzini.

"No tired." She brushed this away. "But is enough
for tonight. We watch television." She reached out to
pat my hand affectionately. "And no mind I nod, you
hear? Stay with me till Rosa comes." Mama *listened*
to TV.

TV reception was poor because of a storm which
was blowing up. I tried first one channel, then another, finding snow everywhere. Mama was already nodding. But she'd pointedly instructed me to stay until
Rosa arrived to help her to bed. I assumed she'd

arranged a time with Giuseppe. I turned off the set,
sat back in my chair, listened to the wind whipping
through the trees with near-gale force.

Outdoors, a car was rolling out of the garage. Below, I could hear the men's voices, discussing the
weather. They were anxious now that business was
out of the way to be driven to the airport. I gathered
that Nino was driving them.

Minutes after the men left, Rosa arrived. She
smiled expansively, waved me on my way, then
moved to Mama's side.

"Signora, is late," I heard Rosa crooning as I left
Mama Mazzini's sitting room. "Time for bed, Signora."

I locked my door securely. Locked all the windows.
The trees were bending beneath the heavy winds
outside. And now the rain was beginning to fall.
Usually, I relish falling asleep while rain beats the
earth outdoors. There's something deliciously satisfying about being warm, dry, cozy, when the elements
are at war.

I went straight to bed, stifled a yawn as I drew the
summer blankets snugly about my shoulders. The
temperature must have dipped at least ten degrees. I
stretched, feeling oddly relaxed, *safe*, with my doors
and windows locked and that storm brewing outdoors. My last thought as my eyes closed was of
compassion for the sentry on duty. Certain he would
be on duty, despite the weather.

I awoke—considerably later—to the sound of a
shutter hitting monotonously against an outer wall.
Not on my windows, I identified the location. On the
floor below. I lay starkly awake now, listening to the
jarring sound of that shutter banging repeatedly. Why
didn't somebody fasten it?

Thunder rocked the outdoor blackness, building
one rending sound upon another. Mountain thunder,
particularly ominous. I groped for the lamp beside
my bed, flipped on the switch. Another clap, seeming
to shake the castle. Wow, that was a bad one!

I shivered slightly in the chill of the storm, though

reassured by the light. A robe, my mind dictated. I
left the bed, went to the closet to pull down the furry
red mandarin robe, pulled it about me. In no mood—
now—for sleep.

With morbid curiosity, I crossed to a window,
gingerly parted the drapes. Retreated in alarm as
lightning zigzagged across the sky. This storm would
be with us for quite a while. Oh, why didn't somebody tie up that shutter? The repetitious banging was
unnerving. What about the night patrol—why didn't
he take care of the shutter?

I settled myself in the chair most distant from the
windows and the celestial display, picked up a magazine. Fully awake. It might have been high noon. I
wasn't likely to go back to sleep until the storm
subsided.

I flipped the pages of the magazine without seeing
anything. Hearing the claps of thunder. Painfully conscious of the lightning streaking across the sky. Then
something—not quite of the storm—snapped me into
alertness.

A strange sound. A rending sound. My eyes located
the source. My heart thumped insanely. The bronze
statue of the Virgin Mary, set in an alcove above my
bed, was falling! Pulling away from its base!

Another clap of thunder, like a Wagnerian background for the descent of the statue. I stifled a
scream. The statue was falling onto my bed! Where I
was supposed to be this moment! Death—certain
death—if I had been lying in that bed. Death, pro-
grammed for me.

CHAPTER

12

Slowly, my throat tightening, I approached the gaping emptiness on the wall, where seconds ago the magnificent bronze statue of the Virgin Mary had stood. My mind refused to accept the supposition that the statue, weighing probably sixty pounds, had fallen of its own volition. Precisely at the time when I would be expected to be sleeping soundly!

Shivering, I inspected the prone statue. If I'd been lying where it had fallen, I would be dead now. I lived because a shutter slid loose from in its moorings in the midst of a thunderstorm.

Why had the statue fallen? My hands trembling—but my mind determined to seek the mechanics of my brush with death—I removed the lampshade from my bedside lamp so that the light would cast more brightness on the alcove behind the bed. I was certain this was more than a warning—this was an attempt at murder!

I moved closer. My eyes inched along the circlet where the statue had stood. Chisel marks, there at the rear. I would swear to that. Someone had deliberately loosened the base of the statue.

I always locked the door, I told myself naively. But when did a locked door defy a criminal, my mind cynically shot back? Someone had entered my rooms, loosened the statue. Still, how could they be sure it would fall during the hours that I slept?

Again, my eyes intently searched the alcove. Seeking some clue. And then, with shattering suddenness,

I knew how this attempt on my life had been engineered. I spied a tiny hole, hardly a quarter of an inch in diameter. The hole had been replastered on the other side of the wall, to disguise the attempt at murder. But a faint dust of plaster lingered. *The hole had been bored just recently.*

It was all diagramed in my mind now. Someone— who?—had slid a steel bit through that tiny hole, and from the other side of the wall hammered the statue from its base. With the thunderstorm as a cover! Expecting me to be the recipient of that deadly weight, and instantly replastering the hole.

I straightened up, thinking hard. What was on the other side of this wall? Who would have access? The castle linen room, my mind pinpointed. Anyone could gain access. Still no answers—

I edged away from the bed, not bothering even to restore the lampshade. Tomorrow would be time enough. I'd spend the rest of the night on the sofa in the sitting room, I told myself grimly. Safe, for tonight. Whoever had thrust that statue upon my bed must be triumphantly sure that I was lying dead—or near death.

I switched on the lamps in the sitting room, re-turned—squeamishly—to the bedroom to turn off the lamp by the bed. The thunder still rumbled heavily outdoors. The lights in the sitting room flickered for a moment. A flashlight, my mind ordered. I groped in a drawer for the compact flashlight I'd brought along with me.

I was halfway to the sitting room when the lights blacked out. A power failure somewhere. Clutching my flashlight, I followed its beam to the sofa, settled myself there for the rest of the night. By the time the power was restored, the first grey streaks of dawn splashed across the sky. Only then did I relax sufficiently to fall asleep again.

I awoke early, stiff from sleeping tensely on the narrow area of the sofa. Cold, despite the furry robe.

Immediately, I was assaulted by the horror of last
night. Sat up quickly, while memory drenched me.

All right, dress, get out of these rooms. Tell Giuseppe what happened last night. Just the bare facts.
Let him—let Mama Mazzini—arrive at conclusions.
Morbidly, I left the sofa, hurried into the bedroom,
bathed now in comforting daylight. Still, it was a
fresh shock to see the heavy bronze Madonna lying
prone across my bed.

I slid into warm slippers, my feet two chunks of ice,
reached into a drawer for fresh underthings, into my
closet for the persian blue slack suit for this unseasonably cool morning. Into the bathroom, the door shut
against the ugliness on my bed.

I switched on the heating panel, grateful for this
sybaritic luxury. Impatient now to be out on the road,
pedaling toward my rendezvous spot. Tony would be
upset about this. What did I do now. Run? Logic told
me to run. Still, how could I be sure the attempts on
my life would stop if I ran? I must find out who it
was that wished me dead.

I dressed swiftly, took a final glance at myself in
the mirror, a ribbon holding my hair back from my
face. The blue slack suit vastly flattering. Nothing in
my appearance this morning betrayed the horror of
last night. Still, someone in the castle would be startled to discover I was still alive.

I walked self-consciously from my rooms, down the
corridor to the wide, circular staircase. This early—
just past seven thirty—there would nobody moving
about downstairs except for Lucia and Giuseppe. I
started down the lower floor corridor, toward the
breakfast room, spotted Giuseppe in the customarily
closed-up library. He was diligently polishing the
huge, oval conference table.

"Giuseppe—" I paused at the threshold.

"Si, Signorina?" He glanced up inquiringly.

"There was an—accident in my room last night." I
saw the shock in his eyes, the instant alertness. "The
statue over the bed came loose, tumbled over. Fortu-

nately, I'd been disturbed by the storm. I was across the room." Giuseppe was white, his eyes fastened on me. "I slept the rest of the night on the sofa—" Suddenly, I was breathless. Giuseppe, too, realized this had been an attempt on my life.

"Signorina, you should have called," he stammered. "I would have prepared another room for you."

"I didn't want to disturb anybody at that hour." I forced a smile. Did Giuseppe know I suspected a murder attempt? Some instinct warned me to pretend I didn't know. "It was one of those once in a thousand years accidents," I continued glibly.

"The Signora will be upset," Giuseppe said unhappily.

"Do we have to tell her?"

"Si, Signorina," he said positively, and sighed heavily. "The Signorina must know."

I went on out to the breakfast room. Lucia waddled in with coffee and pastry fresh from the oven, her eyes plainly telling me she knew nothing of what happened last night. But could I have suspected Lucia? I must suspect everyone, my mind exhorted.

Minutes later, while I ate Lucia's superb pastry without even tasting it, I saw Giuseppe in the kitchen, talking in a low voice to Lucia. I heard the low, shocked exclamation that escaped her, saw the excitement—the fear—on her face. Giuseppe was telling her about the fallen statue.

I ate quickly, anxious to be out on the bicycle, en route to Tony. By the time I returned, I thought uneasily, the whole domestic staff would be whispering about last night's near fatality. Victor would be back tonight. What would he think? My heart pounded in recurrent recall.

I saw the alarm in Lucia's eyes when I exchanged a few words with her while I brought the bicycle out of the storeroom. I smiled determinedly, not letting on that, inwardly, I was terrified.

The outdoors was lush after the heavy rainfall, the air fragrant with the scent of newly mown grass. On a morning such as this it was difficult to realize that, hours ago, I'd missed death because of an unlatched shutter.

I pedaled down the path to the walled avenue. From habit my eyes sought Antonio. He wasn't in sight. Probably on the other side of the grounds. But this morning my sole interest lay in meeting Tony. He was to be a mile down the road, sufficiently distant from the farmhouse so that no one would notice us.

I pedaled with a sense of urgency, my eyes focused on the ribbon of road ahead. Involuntarily, I smiled. I spied Tony, motorbike parked by a tree while he slouched on the grass. There, he saw me. He was waving.

I waved back exuberantly, feeling a surge of security at his nearness. Tony scrambled to his feet, started to walk toward me.

"Bright and early," he said, reaching for my hand when I'd dismounted. "Beautiful in blue—" His eyes caressing me. "No problems?" The casualness in his voice contradicted by the seriousness in his eyes.

"Problems," I admitted. Instantly, he tensed.

"Such as?" he demanded quietly, but his hand tightened on mine.

Striving for calm, I explained about the statue. Omitting nothing. The hole in the wall. The plaster dust. The chisel marks about the base of the statue.

"Somebody meant to murder you." Tony was pale, his eyes incensed. "I don't understand—it doesn't fit in with the picture."

"Tony, what picture?" I probed. "What's going on here? Tony, I have a right to know."

Tony hesitated.

"Andrea, trust me," he pleaded. "I can't tell you yet—" He stared unhappily into space. "Honey, trust me."

"All right." But I was operating on emotion.

"Who was at the castle last night?" Tony asked me.

"Victor's away—he had to go down to the city to have his cast repaired." Did Tony know about Victor?

Yes. "Nino went out last evening, but he returned quite late. I heard the car. Oh, Aldo drove Victor into the city—he was away, too."

"And the servants, except for Giuseppe, sleep over the garage," Tony remembered.

"Tony, I don't know if it means anything—" Was I doing right to tell Tony about last night's guests? Yes, tell Tony everything, I ordered myself impulsively. "There were guests last night—three men were met at the airport by Nino. He drove them back just before the storm broke."

"What about Carlo?" Tony asked quickly. "Any word about his arrival?"

"Nothing else. But wait—" I thought about Giuseppe this morning, in the library. "The library is obviously used for conferences. Giuseppe was in there this morning, polishing the table. Would that suggest something, Tony?"

"It would," Tony said briskly. "The arrival of the Don—the big meeting."

"Tony, are you involved in this cigarette company merger?" I had a right to know. Didn't I? "Or in the land acquisition?" I churned to know Tony's part in this scene.

"I'm involved with the cigarette company merger," Tony conceded with a slow smile. "Andrea, I can't answer questions just yet—but there's nothing illegal about my operation. Believe me, honey," he emphasized. "But what's this about land acquisition?"

"I heard Nino on the telephone," I explained. "He was talking about the deed to fifty-five thousand acres they'd acquired—and another fifty thousand acres available. Nino was furious when he realized I'd overheard this."

Tony whistled sharply.

"That's a lot of land!" He frowned slightly. "Where is it, Andrea? Did he say?"

"In the Islands. Whatever that means." I sensed that Tony knew.

"Andrea, try to stay clear of Nino," Tony ordered

somberly. "My radar tells me he could be the one. Too many signs pointing in his direction."

"But Tony, he couldn't have had anything to do with the snake in my room," I pointed out. "And those notes?" I shook my head doubtfully.

"These attempts to frighten you—" Tony carefully refrained from saying "murder." "They don't fit into any logical formula."

"Do things ever?" I burst out impatiently.

"Later, we'll understand." He squeezed my hand reassuringly, but his eyes were troubled. "If I were in my right mind, I'd throw you on my motorbike and ride straight away from here. So far they'd never find you."

"I won't be safe until we know who's out to kill me," I said with a stoicism I wasn't feeling. But along with fear was a monumental curiosity—and indignation. "The only way to find out is to stay here." But I shivered. *How* would we find out?

"Andrea, the minute you can manage it, tell Carlo Mazzini the whole scene about the statue. About the snake, and the second note. Leave out nothing. I have a hunch he'll nail the creep and stop all this insanity. Mazzini can't afford a murder in the castle. Not with this merger breathing down his neck."

"Tony, I don't see how I fit into all this," I burst out in frustration. "What do I have to do with a secret business merger?"

"Nothing that I can see," Tony admitted honestly. "If Carlo Mazzini had been concerned about your being a leak to the outside, he wouldn't have hired you. I don't know—" He shook his head, frowning uneasily. "But the old radar still tells me we must watch Nino." Tony checked his watch now. "Andrea, I have to cut out," he said apologetically. "I'll see you here in the morning. Okay?"

"Sure." I smiled mockingly. "I have no other pressing social engagements." My tone flip, my eyes somber. I was disappointed that Tony was rushing off this way.

Tony leaned forward to kiss me with an urgency
that was startling. And then he was on the motorbike,
charging off with a burst of speed. Was I wrong in
trusting Tony this way? *Was he using me?*

When I returned to the castle, Rico was at the huge
wrought-iron gates, brushing on fresh black paint.
Carlo Mazzini must be expected shortly, for this top-
level meeting. Giuseppe polishing the conference table, Rico painting the entrance gates.

My first instinct was to turn the bike around, try to
catch up with Tony somehow, to report this new hint
of an imminent meeting. But Tony wouldn't be there.
He hadn't even given me a phone number where he
could be reached. . . .

At the castle, I put away the bicycle, strolled into
the breakfast room. Sophia was talking in a furtive
whisper to Lucia. Both started at my appearance.
They knew about the bronze Madonna.

"Breakfast come quick, Signorina," Lucia said, her
eyes a blend of compassion and fear. "You sit."

I sat at the breakfast room table, pushing aside the
butter-yellow cafés as I always did, for a better view
of the outdoors—the lush greenness, the imposing
mountains in the distance. But this morning I gazed
without seeing. My mind churned with questions.

Tony said there was nothing illegal about his being
here. That he was involved in the merger with the
cigarette company. Which meant, I interpreted, that
he was working for a rival firm. I remembered reading articles about industrial espionage. Was Tony
engaged in this kind of work? Was it dangerous?

What about us—Tony and me? Was I being incred-
ibly naive? Again, guilt stirred in me. I was being dis-
loyal to Carlo Mazzini when I fed information to Tony.

What about afterward? Would I see Tony again? I
was in love with him—no doubts in my mind about
that. What about Tony? Was *he* in love with me—or
using me?

Lucia brought my breakfast, poured coffee for me.

We made the routine morning small talk, though both
of us wore strained smiles. I ate Lucia's epicurean
scrambled eggs and sausages without tasting. From
habit, poured myself a second cup of coffee when I'd
drained the first.

I glanced up in astonishment when the faint whirr
of the chair told me Mama was being wheeled into
the breakfast room.

"Coffee for me, Giuseppe," she ordered tersely
when he'd positioned her at the table. "One more cup
won't kill me, Giuseppe," she insisted as he opened
his mouth to object. From the tone of her voice, I
knew Giuseppe had told her about last night.

Mama waited until we were alone before she spoke
about my brush with death.

"Andrea, when Giuseppe tell me this morning, I am
so upset. Such an accident to happen, here at the
castle!" She crossed herself, eyes closed for a moment.
"Is a sign, Andrea—from the Blessed Mother herself.
A sign you must leave the castle!"

"But an accident like that won't ever happen
again," I protested gently.

I was watching her carefully. *Mama Mazzini didn't
believe it was an accident.* She was terrified for me.
Had she sent Giuseppe to inspect? Had he seen the
hole? Anyone searching for evidence must find it.

"The Blessed Mother—she tell you this way,"
Mama said heavily. "Andrea, for me is wonderful to
have you here at the castle. I enjoy. But not when is
like this—" She gestured expressively with the heavily
veined hands.

I wavered, with Mama's eyes holding mine hypnot-
ically. Knowing she was right. That there was logic
on her side. Yet I rebelled at being driven away.
Away from Tony, my mind taunted. Why didn't Tony
urge me to leave? Wouldn't a man in love do that?
Suddenly, my heart was thumping away.

"When Mr. Mazzini comes up to the castle, let me
talk about it with him," I hedged persuasively. "If he
thinks I should leave, then, of course, I will. . . ."

I felt such a sense of loss at the prospect of running away from the castle. Where would I go? Back to the college town, to wait for school to open. Away from Tony. *What about Tony?* Why did he allow me to remain in danger? Tony knew it was dangerous for me to remain at the castle.

Mama gazed earnestly at me with her failing sight.

"Yes, Andrea," she said softly. "When Carlo come, we talk. He will see is wrong for you to stay. Nothing must happen to you, Andrea." Her voice trembled with determination.

We finished our coffee, and I was allowed to wheel Mama into the small salon for our reading session. As I turned the chair into the room, I spied Giuseppe at the other end of the corridor, watching me with sharp anxiety. Not because I had usurped his place, temporarily, behind Mama's chair. Because he feared for my life.

We read the current newspaper with detailed thoroughness this morning. It was as though Mama was involving herself in this impersonal news, to refrain from dwelling on the castle happenings. When I laid aside the newspaper, Mama talked, ramblingly, about her girlhood in the small town near Catania. She was still talking when Giuseppe came in to tell us that Lucia was ready to serve luncheon.

Nino was at the table already, involved in an airline timetable. A knot tightened in the pit of my stomach when his arrogant eyes grazed me before they settled on his great-aunt. It was the first eye-to-eye encounter with Nino since I'd slapped him, in Victor's presence.

Was it Nino who contrived for the statue to fall on my bed? Tony suspected him. The motive was there. Discount the notes, the snake—this had all the earmarks of Nino Santini. But how did we prove it?

I concentrated on luncheon. Not actually hungry but knowing I must go though the motions of eating. And the plate was a safe destination for my eyes.

"Nino, what do you hear from Gina?" Mama inquired. "And the children?"

"Gina's okay." Nino was sullen. "She's got the kids with her out at the Long Beach house." He shot a defiant glance at me. The fabulously expensive Long Beach house was a source of deep pride with Nino. "They're going to Gina's folks for a few days next week."

Mama pointedly inquired about the children, one by one. Offered news about their multitude of cousins. A miracle that Mama remembered so many names! Mama was filling in what could have been an oppressive silence about the table.

Halfway through luncheon, Nino received a call. He rose swaggeringly to his feet, apologized for leaving the table, a courtesy that seemed grotesquely foreign to his nature, and strode off, chin high with self-inflated importance.

"I miss Victor," Mama said, at a lull in the conversation. "I am glad he comes back tomorrow."

"Yes." I smiled my agreement.

"Is a good boy, my Victor." Mama suddenly seemed exhausted. She was upset, recurrently, about the differences between Victor and his grandfather. Mama looked sharply at me now. Wondering about Victor's interest in me? I stirred self-consciously. Victor was quite overt about his interest in me. "Andrea, you drive?" Mama asked as Nino strode back into the dining room.

"Yes ..."

"You do an errand for me this afternoon?" Mama smiled ingratiatingly. "Will be a change for you to get away—"

"I'd love to do your errand," I acquiesced quickly.

"Aldo not here, so you drive into the village, to candy store. Buy chocolates for me." Mama was pleased at this connivance—she knew I was uptight about Nino, I might work off some of my tension away from the castle for a while. Did Mama suspect Nino? I glanced sharply at her. Mama was too loyal to the family to give way to such suspicions. "Maybe you like to do shopping?" Mama pursued. "You need money?"

"Thanks, I have enough for whatever shopping I might do."

"Take whatever car you like," Mama urged. "The red Mercedes Benz?" she offered with pride.

"The Volvo," I decided, more at home with a less flamboyant car. Victor's favorite, usually. I ignored Nino's smirk.

" I tell Giuseppe give you key—he takes care when Aldo is not here. Have yourself a good time, Andrea," Mama urged with satisfaction. "Go any time you like."

As soon as Mama was wheeled up to her rooms, I went to my own. The early morning unseasonable cold had given way to summer splendor. I was impatient to change into one of my summer shifts. I was glad that Mama had assigned me this errand. It would lift my spirits to leave the castle for a while.

Downstairs again, I sought out Giuseppe, who walked with me to the garage, where the keys were hung on a board.

"The Volvo, Signorina," he said, handing me a key. "Is plenty of gas. Aldo fill each time the car comes back to garage."

"Thank you." I smiled warmly, slid behind the wheel, fitted the key into the ignition. Feeling pleased about this excursion. Wishing, wistfully, that I might encounter Tony in the village.

I drove slowly down the long, walled avenue to the gates, remembering the shock that hit me when Rico halted me at the gates that first time I attempted to go for a walk beyond the castle walls. I braked as I approached the cottage, waved casually to Rico. He stared sharply at me, ambled over to the gates, unlocked them, shoved them wide.

"Okay." He was as surly as usual. Armed as usual. My eyes had compulsively sought out the holstered gun. "Go on—" He waved me on. Giuseppe had called down that I was leaving in a car, I guessed. The security was as tight as ever.

I remembered the route to the village, though Giuseppe had painstakingly retraced it verbally for me. A right at the gates. I swung right, feeling a strange freedom behind the wheel, beyond the castle gates. Then this sharp descent around the side of the mountain.

After a few hundred yards, the road leveled off. I knew it would remain this way for about a quarter of a mile, before another, much sharper descent. It was good to be behind the wheel of a car again. I hadn't driven since last summer, when my job included picking up ten pre-schoolers in our day camp program.

The road was lightly traveled. So far I hadn't passed another car. The delivery men, the milkmen, had been here early in the morning. No bus passed this way. The houses were far apart. My eyes swept the panorama before me with enjoyment for the moment. Not too many miles, north, the way I was headed, lay Canada. There was a kind of excitement in living close to the border of another country.

Victor had said he'd gone skiing in the Laurentians last winter. It would be fun to run up to Quebec City for several days, when I finished my assignment here, I thought carelessly, living in this second. And then reality gripped hold of me, and my hands tightened cautiously at the wheel.

I was approaching the steep descent—the one Victor kidded about using as a ski slope in winter. My foot left the gas pedal for the brake. I pushed down, gently at first, then with more force, alarm tugging at me.

What was the matter? I was going too fast! I jammed the pedal to the floor. Still the car traveled at breakneck speed. What was wrong with the brakes? And, suddenly, I knew! Someone had tampered with them! What could I do? How did I stop?

I clutched the wheel, my foot pounding at the brakes. Terror closing in about me. I was going to crash! At this speed, on this mountain road! *What could I do?*

CHAPTER

13

I clung to the wheel, my foot senselessly pumping at the brake. Frantically, I tried the handbrake. It refused to hold. Again, I pumped at the footbrake, with no results. My heart pounding, I knew death stretched out waiting for me below.

"Andrea!" Tony's voice, insanely close. *Where was he?* "Andrea!"

I turned my head, startled to find a blue Valiant racing up to me, Tony at the wheel! Almost on a level with me now. What was he doing? How could he help?

"Tony, the brakes!" I cried out. "They won't hold!"

"Shoot into low gear, Andrea!"

"All right—" Still, the car raced, the descent too sharp for the motor to respond to the change of gear.

"Andrea, swerve sharply to the right, just below!" Tony shouted. "Where the road levels out. Before the next drop! Now, Andrea—now!"

My reflexes responding to the command in his voice, I made the sharp right, plowing into the underbrush, crashing into a tree. Tony's car moving in beside me, positioning to keep me from tipping. The Volvo miraculously still. Subconsciously, I noted that Tony's right fender was a mess.

I sat there, clinging to the wheel, too shaken to budge. Tony thrust open the door to the Valiant, hurried over to me.

"Andrea," he called out anxiously. "Andrea, are you all right?"

"Fine—" My breathing was labored, my voic husky. "Oh, Tony!" I shivered, imagining how I migh have been if Tony hadn't intervened.

"Honey, it's all right," he soothed, sitting beside m reaching for my hands. "Close," he admitted ruefully searching my face. His eyes trying for reassuranc "But you're not hurt. That's what counts."

"Oh, Tony, Tony—" I threw myself into his arm clinging to him, my heart pounding against his ches "I thought it was all over for me. I couldn't see an way out—"

"I was parked a few hundred yards from the castl gates," Tony explained. "Well concealed. I didn't rea ize it was you at the wheel until the car was past. didn't want to catch up with you—I had a crazy ide you might have been followed. Then I realized wha was happening." His arms tightened about me.

"Tony, somebody must have tampered with th brakes! The cars are kept in perfect condition—Aldo' constantly working on them." I was still trembling "But even the handbrakes were shot!"

"That figures. The fluid drained from the foot brakes, the handbrakes jammed. You'd be in bad trouble on these sharp descents into the village. An drea, who knew you were taking the car?"

"Mama Mazzini," I recalled slowly. "Giuseppe. Oh, and Nino—he was at the table when Mama asked me to drive into the village. She asked which car I'd like to take. I specifically said the Volvo."

"So Nino knew which car to sabotage," Tony said tautly. "Andrea, it has to be Nino!"

"How do we prove it?" I asked unsteadily.

"I'm not sure that we can," Tony conceded. "But we'll nab Nino—I promise you that—one way or another." Tony sighed heavily. "Andrea, I must level with you now. I'm not Antonio's grandson—" He was reaching into his pocket, pulling forth his wallet. "Here—" Somberly, his eyes watching me, he extend- ed his identification.

I took the black leather wallet, turned it around so

hat I could read. Anthony Sims, FBI! I sat there, staring numbly, reading and re-reading the identification information. Yet I'd never—even from the beginning—entirely believed that he was Antonio's grandson, studying agriculture at a small college in Alabama.

"At least, you're still Tony." I tried to be flip. "I'd never get used to calling you something else." My eyes focused on his face. "Tony, what's this all about?"

"We don't know why someone at the castle is trying to murder you, Andrea," he said quietly. "We know other things. That Carlo Mazzini is top-level Mafia—"

"That courtly old gentleman?" I stared in disbelief. "Carlo Mazzini? Nino, I could believe—but—" I shook my head in bewilderment.

"Carlo Mazzini heads one of the most important families operating on a national level. The castle—it cost over a million—was bought for secret meetings, as well as for a home for Mama Mazzini. This is the headquarters for very private, very important Mafia business." Tony leaned forward urgently. "Andrea, we know a top-level meeting is coming up—one that will affect this entire nation. *We must know who is at that meeting*. Andrea, that's why you're at Castle Mazzini."

"Tony, I don't understand." My head was whirling.

"You will," he promised gently. "We'll leave your car here. If mine's still operating, we'll go where you can hear the whole story."

Tony moved out of the car, helped me out on his side. I was still shaking inwardly. He held my hand tightly in his while we made our way to the blue Valiant. Tony settled me comfortably, made his way around to the driver's seat, then turned the ignition key. The motor caught right away. The car was all right. Carefully, Tony backed out onto the road again.

"There's a small house down the road, back in the

woods. We use that as headquarters while we're on
this operation," Tony explained.

"Tony, what did you mean when you said—that's
why you're at the castle?"

"We finagled to have you hired for the job," Tony
admitted. "We've been watching the Mazzini family
for over a year, praying for some break. We knew
Carlo was at the college, inquiring for a student to
read to his mother until she goes in for surgery. Here
was the break we thought would never come along—
our chance to smuggle someone inside the castle itself."

"But Tony, I knew nothing—how did you expect
me to help?"

Tony's hand left the wheel to squeeze mine for a
moment.

"I almost killed the whole scene. When I saw what
was happening to you, I wanted you out of it." So
Tony hadn't been using me. Shaken as I was, I felt a
surge of happiness at this reassurance. "Ted Hamilton
—my chief—insisted we play it out. I've been stationed
on twenty-four-hour duty right outside the castle.
Sleeping in the car. We have another man stationed
on the other side of the gates."

"Tony, I don't understand," I stammered. My mind
churned with unspoken questions. "How did you
finagle to have me hired?"

"We approached Dean Benedict to push you for
the job. We explained the urgency. Actually, there
was a male teacher contracted for next year, with a
background in languages. Benedict was on the point
of contacting him for the job when we moved in."

"Why did you want me?" I persisted. "Why not the
new teacher?"

Tony's face tightened.

"I'll let Ted explain that," he said quietly. "I'd
rather he told you—"

We swung off the road, followed a half-mile private
dirt road to a summer house set in the midst of the
woods. Before we came to a full stop, two men,

rmed, strode forward to clear us. They grinned, vaved, when they recognized Tony.

"Come on, Andrea."

We scrambled out of the car, walked toward the ultra-modern summer house, Tony's hand at my arm as we walked up the stairs onto the deck. There must have been some rigged-up signal because the door swung open before we arrived there.

"Troubles?" A tall, clean-cut man with probing eyes held the door wide for us to enter.

"Somebody drained the brake fluid from her car," Tony explained. "It was close—"

"I'd be dead if Tony hadn't told me what to do," I blurted out.

"Come in, have some coffee. Oh, I'm Ted Hamilton." He smiled, his eyes compassionate. "I always keep fresh coffee perking."

Tony and I sat down on the low, modern sofa. Ted went off to the kitchen area, which followed without divider from the living room-dining area. Ted poured coffee into three mugs, brought them on a hammered aluminum tray to the table before the sofa.

"Okay," Ted said briskly, when I was sitting back sipping gratefully at the strong black coffee. "How much does she know?"

"That we connived with Benedict to place her in the castle," Tony reported. "She knows about Mazzini. That there's a meeting coming up—and we have to know who attends."

"Andrea." Ted leaned forward. "You're our one chance of tying up this whole business. We know the Mafia is deeply involved in selling narcotics. They're buying into a cigarette company, for cover—but their money comes from drugs. You've told us they've bought fifty-five thousand acres in the Islands—"

"I heard Nino say this over the phone," I specified uneasily.

"Fifty-five thousand acres for growing drugs," Ted Hamilton pinpointed brusquely. "To flood this country with that rottenness while they pad their pockets! We

let this move go through, we'll face the worst invasio
of drugs this country has yet encountered—and it'
been grim enough so far!"

"But how can I help?" I gazed fearfully at Tony
Wanting an out. Terrified! "They're trying to kill me
already—"

"That's the part we can't figure out," Ted admitted
reflectively. "But Andrea—" His voice was suddenly
commanding. "We know you'll help us."

"Why?" I put down the coffee mug before I could
spill coffee on the elegant modern glass coffee table.

"Because, Andrea," Ted Hamilton said very quietly,
"Carlo Mazzini ordered your father's death."

"It was an accident," I whispered, cold as a chunk
of ice. "He was lost in the desert—he died of exposure." There were the columns in the newspapers
—they all said that!

"No." Ted rejected this. "Your father was in Las
Vegas, tracking down the Mafia gambling tie-in. He
was closing in on them—they knew this. Nobody is
ever killed by the Mafia in Las Vegas—people simply
'get lost in the desert and die of exposure.' Your
father was in contact with us. He was about to break
this gambling syndicate—and so they had to kill
him."

"Oh, no. Oh, no!" Suddenly, the whole ugliness was
back, turning me sick. The horror of the police, coming to tell me my father, my wonderful father, was
dead. "Oh, no, no!"

Tony reached for my hand, squeezed hard.

'Andrea, we know how rough this is on you. But
we know you'll want to help. Because of your father."

"We've watched you ever since your father's
death," Ted said gently. "We were afraid for a while
that they might try to harm you. We watched to
insure your safety. And then, with one of those
crazy twists of fate, Carlo Mazzini was approaching
the college—*your college*—about a reader for his
mother. Antonio tipped us off to that."

"Antonio hates the Mafia," Tony explained. "He's

worked with us for years. But, of course, Antonio
never gets inside the castle. And he must be off the
grounds by five."

"We requested Dean Benedict to make a point of
playing down your last name—lest Mazzini be suspicious. He's always referred to you as 'the student' or
'this young lady.' Also, he was instructed to plant the
false information that your parents were traveling in
Europe, to dispel any suspicions of a connection between Andrea Grant and Roger Grant." Ted leaned
forward earnestly. "Andrea, this is a tremendous
break for us—if you'll play along. We know that Carlo
Mazzini is setting up the largest drug syndicate ever
operated in the United States—a confederation of the
big families, with himself at the head. But we must
know which men are specifically involved. That way,
we have a chance of nailing them, bringing them to
trial."

"I have one bit of information," I offered unsteadily. "I don't know if it's of any importance."

"What's that, Andrea?" Ted was watching me
keenly.

"A visitor showed up one evening—and Mama
Mazzini arranged for me to have dinner upstairs with
her and Victor. Giuseppe referred to him as the Congressman—and later, Nino also. I saw him, from my
bedroom balcony—"

"Did you recognize him?" Ted exchanged a sharp
glance with Tony.

"No," I conceded apologetically. "But he looked
familiar. I've seen him on television or in the newspapers."

"The family must be upset over the new bills aimed
against the drug traffic," Tony guessed. "They're
going after Washington wheels. Andrea, would you
recognize a photograph?"

"I think so. . . ." I concentrated, bringing the Congressman's face into my mind. "Oh, yes."

"Ted, do we have photos here?"

"We'll get them," Ted promised. "Within twenty-four hours."

"What do you want me to do?" My voice was taut with determination. *I must help the FBI.* For my father I had to help them. If the FBI couldn't imprison Carlo Mazzini and his mob for murder, then it must be for dope traffic. I owed my father this! "How can I help?" My eyes moved from Tony to Ted, saw the flash of answering excitement in them.

"By identifying the men who come to that summit meeting." Ted leaned forward, his eyes holding mine. "We'll know who to watch—we'll be able to pick them up, Andrea. Maybe six or eight of the top men among the families. We can't be sure of the date."

"Soon," I said recklessly. "Tonight, tomorrow, the next. This morning Giuseppe was polishing the conference table. Rico was painting the gates. There's a feeling in the castle . . ."

"They'll come in rented limousines," Ted continued with ironic humor. "Rented so there will be no tails on them. Rented in the names of lackeys. They'll drive up, one by one, into the castle grounds—and you, Andrea—" He took a deep breath. "Sometime during the hours they're there, you must see their faces. Well enough to choose them from our files. When that happens, cut out of the castle fast. Use the bike bit—that's a blessing for our side—"

"She'll have to wait until morning," Tony cautioned. "It's normal then. Everything has to be normal." Tony was scared, for me.

"In the morning," Ted conceded. "Bike down the road—we'll have cars watching steadily. You'll be approached. Ask for identifications," he warned—and I saw Tony frown uneasily. Tony wished, at this moment, that I was out of this. I loved him for that solicitude. "They'll bring you here. You run through our files, pick out the men. Then you'll be driven—right away—down to New York, to remain in hiding until we feel it's completely safe for you to emerge.

It's dangerous," Ted warned. "I can't lie and say it isn't."

"I know." Color stained my cheeks, anger rising in me. Carlo Mazzini had ordered my father's death—and the deaths of how many more men who stood in his way? Carlo Mazzini and his mob were intent on flooding the market with drugs—for profit, to make worse an already untenable condition in the country. "I'll watch for the men," I promised sturdily. "Somehow, I'll manage to get a look at them. Then I'll cut out." I was astonished at the surface cool I managed. Within me churned a blend of fear and fury.

Carlo Mazzini, who was so gentle with his mother, so charming and courtly to me, was a murderer, a wholesaler of heroin, cocaine, LSD, whatever the drug bag offered. I was unconcerned now about the efforts to kill me. Carlo Mazzini was uninvolved in this. Probably, this was the work of somebody at the castle, to whom I presumably presented a threat. Later we would know. What was important now was to avenge my father's death.

Tony and Ted Hamilton were exchanging satisfied glances. They knew that I would make every possible effort to carry out my assignment in this operation.

"I'd better take Andrea back to the car," Tony said slowly. "The less time wasted the better." He turned apologetically to me. "I'm afraid you're going to have to hitchhike into the village. We've got to play this straight."

"That doesn't matter." I smiled faintly. "I've hitchhiked from campus to town often enough."

"All right, Tony, get cracking," Ted urged. "I hope nobody's passed the car and stopped yet. We'd like to have it on record about the pick-up."

"The traffic's light on that road," Tony assured him. "At first glance—just driving past—they'll think the car is parked there. Usual roadside situations—somebody stopping to study a map, catch some rest, walk a dog." Unexpectedly, he grinned. "My car's got

a smashed fender, Ted. We'll have to keep it under
wraps for a few days."

"Take the black Plymouth," Ted instructed, reaching into his pocket for the keys. "Andrea, remember
—we have no way of knowing when the meeting
is going to be held. Suddenly there's going to be
a line-up of black Cadillac limousines. You'll have
to be watching all the time."

"I'll be watching," I promised. "Don't worry about
me." I was cold with apprehension, knowing what I
must do.

Tony drove me back to the Volvo. We passed no
one en route. At the site, Tony held me in his arms
for one poignant, urgent moment—and then he was
reaching over to push open the car door for me.

"Andrea, be careful," he pleaded gently. "Please, be
careful!"

Tony drove off. Feeling frighteningly alone, I took
up my place at the side of the road. Outside the
air-conditioned car, the day was hot, muggy, the sun
unkind. But I stubbornly stood there, perspiration
beginning to bead my forehead, cause my summer
cotton to cling between the shoulderblades. I squinted, watching for the approach of a car.

Castle Mazzini could never be the same to me. I
knew its ugly secret. I understood Victor's tormented
soul. Mama Mazzini—how did she live with the
knowledge?

I remembered the sadness in her eyes, her compul-
sive reminiscences about her girlhood in Sicily, where
her family, peasants, had been the victims of the
Mafiosi. Oh, Mama never used the word, but the
inference was always clear. Her father, a brother, bru-
tally murdered—and no one brought to justice.

Here in the United States, Mama's sons became the
Mafia. To them, a kind of poetic justice in this—but
not to Mama, who couldn't shut her eyes to the
corruption and murder. Victor, knowing, refused to
become part of that world. Mama was glad. His
grandfather couldn't—would never—comprehend.

I straightened up attentively. A vintage Chevy was rumbling along the road, just ahead. I held up a hand in the classic position. The car pulled to a squeaky stop before me. A spare, deeply tanned farmer, smelling of fertilizer, and the barnyard, leaned forward to open the roped-together door.

"Long way to town on a hot day like this. Come on in," he invited with an air of magnanimity.

"Thanks. The brakes on my car jammed—I had to plow into the side of the mountain," I explained as casually as I could manage, and nodded toward the Volvo.

"Lucky you ain't dead," he said with momentary respect for such luck. "New around here?" He was inspecting me cautiously. "Where do you live?"

"I'm working at the Mazzini place for the summer."

He stared sharply at me.

"With them Eye-talians?"

"That's right."

Wow, the disapproval that emanated from him! Did the local folk suspect that Mafia lived in their midst? No, it wasn't that. It was the opulence of the castle, the security which they could hardly understand, and the fact that day workers were invariably of Sicilian origin.

"You Eye-talian?"

"No, I'm not." I smiled slightly.

"We got some Eye-talians in town. Don't mix much. Fellow at the drugstore—he ain't bad."

"He's awfully nice," I concurred. But his wife hated the Mazzinis. What did they owe Carlo Mazzini— what blackness lay festering in their souls? *Poor Victor.*

We drove in silence for the rest of the trip into the village. I sensed that the farmer disapproved of me on the basis of guilt by association. Perhaps he even regretted giving me a lift.

He made a point of pulling up before the drugstore, though I knew there was no phone booth there.

"They got a phone," he said, untying the door for me now. "They can let you use it. No need spendin' money in one of them pay phones—they make all the calls they want for no extra." A mild contempt in his voice for the "Eye-talians," who were newcomers still after eight years in town.

"Thanks for the ride," I said politely, and scrambled from the car.

I explained to the short, heavy man in the white apron that I'd had an accident, saw the alarm glow in his eyes, to be hastily concealed, covered with perfunctory conversation. Yes, of course I could use the phone—anyone from the castle was a privileged guest in his store. Obsequious on the surface, terrified beneath. Knowing—instinctively knowing—that the accident in my car had been induced.

I dialed the castle number, wondering uncomfortably who would drive down for me. Not Nino! Oh, please—not Nino! At the castle, Giuseppe answered the phone. As matter-of-factly as possible, I explained about the car, indicating not an inkling of my suspicions. But I was conscious of the sharp intake of Giuseppe's breath—the tiny, barely perceptible sigh—and I knew he understood this had been another attempt on my life.

"Wait there, Signorina," Giuseppe ordered me carefully. "Aldo will drive in to bring you home."

"I'll be just inside the drugstore," I said. "It's awfully hot outdoors today."

"I will tell Aldo, Signorina," Giuseppe promised, his voice betraying his emotions. Giuseppe, too, knew this had been an attempt at murder.

Aldo would pick me up, my mind replayed Giuseppe's words. That meant Victor must have returned to the castle. Mama Mazzini would tell him about the statue last night—and now this. Mama would say how she was urging me to leave the castle, that it was dangerous for me. But not yet! I couldn't leave until after the meeting.

I couldn't leave until I'd seen those six or eight

men—that black tribunal, which said who was to die and who was to live, which collected their "protection" fees and all the ill-gotten fortunes from gambling and loansharking and prostitution, which prospered on the drugs they were pumping into our country. And now they planned a more infamous drug syndicate than ever, to bring death and misery upon a country that hadn't yet succeeded in coping with this second government. Oh, I wanted to help wipe out this evil, as my father had tried to help!

I stood by the window, staring out at the lightly populated street. The teenagers gathered idly on a corner. A woman loading produce in the trunk of her car. A trio of senior citizens haranguing one another about some headline in the local newspaper.

Behind the immaculate white display counter, the store owner was talking self-consciously, while he scooped up candies for Mama Mazzini, for which he'd already made it clear he would accept no payment. His wife stood hunched over the cash register on the other side of the store, her mouth pursed in anger—because somewhere along the road, Carlo Mazzini had extended his help and they knew not when they'd be called upon to repay.

I was relieved when the black limousine pulled up outside. I ran out, with a swift goodbye for the store owners. I had the impression that the woman was spewing forth a sudden torrent of anger as the door closed behind me.

Aldo held the door for me, politely closed it and slipped behind the wheel again. His face an impassive mask. Did he know about the accident? Giuseppe must have told him.

Now—only now—did I begin to shiver at the prospect of what lay ahead of me. But I must succeed—I couldn't afford to muff this. I thought about my father, murdered—murdered at Carlo Mazzini's orders. And I wondered if I could look at his face again without showing my fury.

The gleaming, black limousine slowed down to a

crawl at the gates. I was conscious of the elegant freshness of the newly applied black paint. To impress Carlo Mazzini's Mafia associates!

Rico ambled forward to swing the gates wide. Aldo drove inside.

"Aldo, wait—" Victor moved toward the car, clumsy in haste.

From the distraught quality in his eyes, I knew Victor had been briefed about last night's falling Madonna. He'd been told about my "accident" in the car. He was buying neither as accidents. *Victor knew.* Not his grandfather—I clung to this—but part of the ugliness behind the high walls that closed off the castle from the rest of the world.

"Andrea—" Victor seated himself beside me, slammed the door shut. "Andrea, I want you to leave the castle." His voice was uneven. "Now. This afternoon. Go to your rooms and pack. I'll go with you while Aldo drives you to the airport."

"Victor, no," I protested. *I couldn't leave.* Not yet. "There's no reason." I tried to be realistic, calm.

"Andrea, do you think I'll allow you to stay, after what's been happening? You mustn't be hurt—I won't permit that!" A vein in his throat was distended in rage. He rebelled against his impotence in the face of his grandfather's wholesale murdering, was determined to intervene for me. "You must pack up, immediately!"

CHAPTER

14

"Victor, I can't just walk out on your great-grandmother," I tried again.

"She understands," Victor insisted wearily. "Andrea, she doesn't want you hurt. She's upset."

"Tomorrow." I clutched at this delay. "Tonight, we'll sit down and talk it over carefully—the three of us. And if you both feel so strongly then—then I'll leave. In two or three days." My eyes avoided a confrontation with his, my heart thumping.

"Tomorrow," Victor stipulated grimly. "I can't go through longer than that." His eyes were sick as he reached out for my hand. "You don't know how I felt when Giuseppe told me about the car. Somebody at the castle means to kill you." Quite suddenly, Victor's eyes went opaque. He was unnerved at having put this into words, within Aldo's hearing. Aldo would report to Nino—we both realized this. I saw the inner conflict within Victor. He was a Mazzini. But Victor hated everything for which the Mazzini family stood, even while he retreated from betraying his own blood. "Tomorrow, Andrea," he said with a brusqueness born of this conflict, "you'll leave the castle."

"All right, Victor," I acquiesced, my words barely audible. Tomorrow, I must find another method of delaying, unless the Don arrived tonight for his summit meeting with the *Mafiosi*. "What about the car?" I asked, anxious to switch to safer ground. "The front's smashed up, I'm afraid. Your Volvo—"

"Not mine," he retaliated—quickly, then smiled ruefully, "I didn't mean to yell. Aldo called a tow truck

175

in the village. It'll be brought out here. Aldo is as good a mechanic as any in the state."

The Mazzinis didn't wish strange mechanics to probe into the cause of the accident. The family couldn't afford rumors, a possible investigation. Not with a Congressman going to bat for them! So many things were becoming clear to me now.

At the castle Victor took me straight to the small salon, where Mama Mazzini waited, her afternoon rest interrupted by my phone call. With a shaky smile, I extended the white and gold-wrapped candy box, which she accepted wordlessly, allowed to rest across her lap. Her eyes, with their failing vision, rested questioningly on Victor.

"Andrea is leaving in the morning," Victor reported tersely.

"Good. That is good." Mama, her heavily lined face showing every one of her eighty-five years, sighed heavily. "All along, I know it not good for Andrea to be here." Mama's eyes clung to me, as though to reassure herself that I was all right.

"*Why?*" I burst forth compulsively. "Who wants me dead? What kind of a threat do I pose?"

Mama stiffened. A wall rose imperiously between us. Mama suspected Nino—but Nino was family and must be protected. But what about those first days here? The absurd notes? The snake? That couldn't have been Nino. He was making his covert pitches. His ego had not yet been damaged.

"So many servants here, Andrea," Mama said, her voice flat. "How we know what goes on in their minds? But these things happen—and I feel, I feel from the beginning this is a bad house for you."

Mama Mazzini, Victor, and I sat for a while, tense with one another yet loath to separate, bound by words that were unspeakable, until Nino swaggered into the room. He leaned over, whispered in his great-aunt's ear.

"*Si*, Nino," She nodded slowly, exhaustedly. "*Si*."

My eyes moved self-consciously about the room,

ghting to avoid a direct confrontation with Nino's. I
ouldn't bring myself to look at him, knowing he
ust have engineered the phony accident. Who did
is dirty work? Aldo? Rico?

For one heated instant, my eyes settled about me. I
embled before the bravado in his eyes, the glint that
aid he'd win out yet. I swung my eyes to Victor,
eeking reassurance there.

"Victor, Andrea," Mama Mazzini said heavily,
hen Nino was gone. "Tonight we will dine together
a my rooms. Is too much for me to come downstairs
gain. I will send Rosa to tell you when it is ready.
Now, Victor, call for Giuseppe. I will go upstairs to
est a while."

Inside my rooms, with the door locked, I stood very
till for a few moments, my mind programming the
nformation collected downstairs. Nino had whispered
o Mama Mazzini. Right after that, Mama told Victor
nd me to have dinner with her in her rooms. *Guests.*
The summit meeting was tonight!

I pulled off my dress, reached into the closet for
nother. Mama expected me to change for dinner—
verything must appear *normal.* I pulled the printed
ersey over my head, my ears straining for the famil-
ar crunch of a car coming up the pebbled driveway.
. must be at the window when the men arrived below
n their rented limousines.

Oh, no! The zipper of my dress was stuck—I
ouldn't move it up or down. Impatiently, I wrenched
at the metal disk, moving the zipper, ripping the
ersey. Take it off, pull down another dress. This time,
ncautiously walking to the window with the replace-
nent in tow, drawing it over my head right there,
oanking on no one's gazing upward.

I smoothed the dress in place, squinted down the
lriveway. Not a car in sight. I hurried into the
oathroom to splash my face with soap and water,
nastily applied fresh make-up. What time is it? Al-

most six! Mama Mazzini will be sending Rosa to c[...]
me to dinner.

Can I play sick? No. I can't risk that—she might [...]
suspicious. Mama belongs to the family. No ris[...]
Andrea. Not with what's at stake.

No car in the driveway yet. Not one. What abo[...]
Carlo? Won't he arrive earlier? What'll I do, if I'[...]
hung up in Mama's rooms all the time those men a[...]
here? But she'll fall asleep when I read to her, sl[...]
always does. I'll get out. *I must.*

I started at the sharp knock on the sitting roo[...]
door.

"One moment," I called out as matter-of-factly as [...]
could manage. At the door, I hesitated from habi[...]
with my hand on the knob. "Who is it?"

"Rosa, Signorina."

I pulled the door wide, strived for casualness.
"Yes, Rosa?"

"The Signora say come to dinner, please." An air [...]
rush about Rosa that told me Lucia was keeping h[...]
running in the preparations for tonight's guests.

"I'll be right there," I promised, and closed the doc[...]
with a faint smile. Tuned in to the sounds outside[...]
a car coming up the driveway.

I raced across the room to a window, peered ou[...]
impatiently. A black limousine was drawing to a sto[...]
below, Nino rushing forward. Carlo Mazzini, imped[...]
cable as always in his three-hundred dollar suit, th[...]
hand-made shirt and tie, emerged from the car. In[...]
side the castle, downstairs, I heard Lucia callin[...]
sharply to Sophia.

"Sophia, *stupido!* The best glasses tonight!"

Nino walked with one massive arm about his uncle[...]
a smug smile on his face as he talked confidentially[...]
his voice too low to carry to me. His uncle nodde[...]
silently in approval.

I stared uneasily down the driveway. Still brigh[...]
daylight at this hour in the summer. Would the other[...]
wait for the cover of dusk? I couldn't wait around t[...]
find out, I rebuked myself. I must go to Mama'[...]

oms this minute. Everything must seem natural. No
spicions.

Still, my heart pounding, I hung at the window.
ow would I manage to see those men? How naive to
pect this to be simple! No chance of standing here,
specting each as he arrived, engraving his image on
y brain.

I listened to the hum of voices downstairs. That
ecial sound of excitement generated by the immi-
nt arrival of important guests. No more stalling. I
ust go down the corridor to Mama's rooms before
e sent someone else for me. To the command din-
r, plotted to keep me out of sight of the guests I
as so determined to view.

In Mama's sitting room, Victor, clutching a pre-
nner martini, sat somberly in a chair by a window,
anning the *New York Times*. Aware, I was cer-
in, of tonight's top echelon meeting—and furious
being caught beneath the same roof. Mama, her
air positioned at the table in readiness for dinner,
pped nervously with one heavily veined hand,
ithout seeming to be aware of this.

Would Carlo Mazzini come up to pay his respects
his mother before the meeting? Apparently not, I
alized when the elevator door opened and Sophia
heeled out the serving cart. Women—even Mama
azzini—took second place to business.

We were being served the dinner that would be
ld for the men, I guessed. One of Lucia's more
mptuous feasts, when food was tasteless in my
outh. An antipasto platter of artichoke hearts, sliced
noked pork, ripe olives, lettuce, tomatoes. Escarole
up, romaine salad, taglierini with chicken livers, a
ntastic roast duck. The table was laden with food,
r three who possessed little appetite.

While I pecked at the crisp duck with its perfect
ange sauce, the limousines began to arrive. My
art pounded as I counted them. One, and then
other, and another. Eight in all. Eight men to
ther in the conference room below, to plot the drug

syndicate which would lead to more deaths amo
the very young, and not so young. To bring grief
helpless families, and to those who would be t
victims of the hooked when their expensive habit se
them into crime.

"You are not eating," Mama chided me unhappi
"Come, Andrea, eat—" Mama's panacea for all ills,
eat.

"I am eating," I insisted, striving to smile. "B
there's so much."

Mama and Victor forced a desultory conversatio
when all of us were attuned to the sounds below
Mama anxious to see her son, Victor mentally co
demning his grandfather, frustrated at his inability t
right what he knew to be wrong.

Downstairs, an all-male symphony—the jumble c
voices, the sounds of drinking, ice cubes clinkin
against glasses, a glass carelessly splintered, to b
instantly swept away.

Victor sat silent over coffee and Mama's favorit
dessert—chilled strawberries sprinkled with cham
pagne. His eyes were brooding, his body restless. Fo
the first time since I'd met him, the cast on his foo
appeared to be a monumental discomfort.

Victor excused himself while Mama and I lingere
over second cups of expresso.

"All right, go rest, Victor," Mama agreed absently
"Andrea will read to me." Her eyes said—for the las
time, Andrea will read to me.

Downstairs, the jumble of voices, the clatter o
glasses ceased. One man was talking, his voice indis-
tinguishable up here. Instinct told me this was the
Don.

How do I get downstairs? *I must.* How can I stay up
here and read to Mama about social events back in
Sicily when the meeting is going on downstairs?
They're counting on me—Tony and Ted. Nobody but
me to see those faces around the conference table!

I read without understanding what I said. Nor was
Mama's mind on the newspaper. She was exhausted

m the tensions of the day. Her head began to nod. I
tched covertly as I read. In minutes she was snor-
g faintly.

I laid aside the newspaper. Mama would stay that
ay, snoring slightly, until Rosa came to nudge her
o semi-wakefulness and help her into bed. Rosa
uld come late tonight, because the meeting down-
irs would be followed by dinner, and Rosa would
standing by. Giuseppe would serve, on such an
casion, assisted by Rosa and Sophia. None of the
y help would be on hand, not at a summit confer-
ce called by Don Carlo Mazzini.

I *must* see those eight strange men about the table.
missed my chance at the window. I had to con-
ve some way to go downstairs and face them
fficiently long to remember each face.

I went to Mama Mazzini, gently prodded her into a
mfortable position. She'd be all right until Rosa
me. Let me walk downstairs and do what must be
ne. Careful, Andrea—*careful.*

I walked noiselessly down the carpeted staircase,
ming in my mind the words which must cover my
pearance. Most important—not to lose my cool. As
as these men knew, I guessed nothing. I was
mbling, unknowingly, into territory where only the
er circle dared to tread.

I started down the corridor, my heart thumping
sanely. My throat tight, a fixed smile on my face.
rlo Mazzini's voice drifted from the library. The
ors were open so that Giuseppe could move freely
and out of the room with drinks. That sonorous
ice was drawing me on.

"We operate the normal trade, as always—we do
t worry about losing money. We will sell the hard
ff, and with this new plan we build ourselves more
stomers for this—because the other is a starter
ug." Triumph in his voice, and I fought down a
ve of sickness. "Now, the new arrangement. As of
day we own controlling stock in the cigarette com-
ny. What we do here is absolutely legitimate. We

start growing the marijuana in the Islands immedia'
ly, to be prepared. We have set up the framework f
the lobbying in Washington. We have the money
put this across. We have certain Congressmen in o
pockets," Carlo boasted smugly, "and when marijua:
is declared legal, we will jump into over-the-count
sale of marijuana cigarettes. Gentlemen, here is t
layout prepared by our advertising agency. The d
sign patent is now being filed by our lawyers
Washington."

Carlo Mazzini reached for a four-color advertisi:
layout, held it aloft. I stared in disbelief. Marijua:
to be sold over the counter, the way Lucky Strikes
Chesterfields are sold today! Carlo Mazzini wooi:
Congressmen with his money, his power, buying lo
byists to help foist this on the American public!

And then he spied me, hovering there in the doc
way.

"What is it, Andrea?" His voice cold steel.

"Excuse me, gentlemen." I tried for ingratiatin
youthful confusion. "The Signora is sleeping. I can
downstairs to borrow a typewriter to write a letter
my parents. I seemed to remember one down here—
My eyes moving with apology from one face to anot
er. Memorizing, ignoring the coldly furious eye
"Please excuse me—"

"Wait, Andrea—" His voice was almost norm
again, almost courtly. "Giuseppe," he called briskl
"Giuseppe!"

Giuseppe came hurriedly forward with stiff ga'
saw me, paled.

"Giuseppe," Carlo Mazzini directed. "The typewri
er over there—" He pointed to the portable I'd r
called seeing earlier. "Please carry it up to the Sign
rina's rooms."

"I'm sorry to be such a nuisance." Play it ingenuou
my mind exhorted. I might—I just might—get awa
with this.

"Our pleasure, Signorina," Carlo Mazzini said wit
his Old World charm. But Nino was livid.

My breathing labored from nervousness, I followed
useppe up the stairs to my rooms. He waited for me
open the door, carried the portable electric to the
sk, with its delicate pictoral marquetry seeming to
ock me tonight.

"Goodnight, Signorina," Giuseppe said quietly. But
s eyes were terrified.

My hand trembling, I pulled a sheet of paper from
e desk, slid it into the typewriter, began a letter:
Dear Mother and Dad—"

I forced myself to type, listening to the sharp stac-
to of the keys in the quietness of the upstairs.
orced myself to compose a coherent letter, lest I be
ced by Carlo Mazzini or one of his associates. In my
ind, I dissected each instant when I stood facing
at group of ten men. They'd been shocked. Fearful
my invasion. Angry that Carlo Mazzini—in his
p-security castle—had allowed this to happen.

Tomorrow, I warned myself, I must wake early,
ke the bike, run! The cars would be there, down the
ad. This nightmare would be over. I would remem-
er each of those faces. Oh, yes—I would remember.

I started at the faint knock on the door, yet feeling
s urgency. Instinct warned me not to call out. I
urried to the door, opened it. Victor, his face dis-
aught, hurried inside, shut the door.

"You little idiot, what did you do?" He was trem-
ling. "Giuseppe came to warn me. *What did you
o?*"

"I went downstairs for a typewriter." I forced a
ewildered smile. "Was your grandfather angry? He
idn't seem to be . . ." Lying to Victor, because how
ould I tell him the truth?

"Andrea, you saw them." His eyes were dark with
nguish. "Do you know what that means? *You know
ho was at the meeting.* Before they're finished
ith dinner, you've got to be out of this house."

Victor had no need to elaborate. I'd seen them—
hey couldn't afford to let me live.

"Victor, how?" The gates were locked. An arme
guard patrolled the grounds. "How?"

Victor squinted in concentration, perspiration bea
ing his forehead, though the night was mounta
cool.

"One way," he decided tensely. "Aldo is in t
garage, checking out the cars for the return trips. Th
other drivers are in a room over the garage, playin
poker. They'll be fed there, later. But nobody will b
leaving for hours," Victor emphasized. "Dinner alway
goes on forever. I'll have to go out to the garage, ca
Aldo outside—"

"Victor, I don't understand—" My head ached wit
the effort to try to follow him.

"Andrea, they're going in to dinner now—the serv
ants will be busy serving. You must sneak ou
through the front—"

"What about the sentry?" I questioned, shivering a
the prospect of running into him. *Still not compre
hending.*

"He'll be on duty outside the dining room window
from now until the men leave the table," Victor ex
plained. "Pick your way across the south gardens, sta
in the shadows when you approach the garage. I'
talk to the sentry for a few minutes, to give you
chance to make it clear, then I'll follow. I'll call Ald
outside, talk to him about driving me to a ginmil
maybe about picking up some girls—" His smile wa
bitter. Victor knew that tonight would forever stan
between us. "While Aldo and I are yakking, yo
sneak into the garage, climb into the back seat of th
Mercedes. You'll find a blanket there—cover yourse
with it. *Keep down, Andrea.* Aldo and I will drive t
the ginmill—" Victor was pulling a wad of bills fror
his pocket, thrusting them at me.

"Victor, no!"

"You'll need money," he insisted brusquely. "Take
cab to the village. Pay him off, take another cab to th
next town. Catch the first bus out of town—an

change for a New York connection. You'll lose any tail that way."

"Victor, what about you?" My voice was a terrified whisper.

His face was taut with determination. His eyes oblique.

"I was with my great-grandmother all evening—Giuseppe and she will attest to that. Except for the short while at a ginmill with Aldo. *We didn't know you were in the back of the car.* Now do exactly as I say," Victor exhorted. "Aldo and I will get into the Mercedes. We'll drive to the ginmill at the edge of the village. When we get out of the car and go into the ginmill, you climb out, Andrea. Run! *Run for your life.*"

"I'd better take a coat." I moved to th
closet, walking in a nightmare.

CHAPTER

15

Victor reached to hold the coat fo
me. I pulled my purse from a drawe
stuffed the bills inside, trembling. Vio
tor reached for me, held me close fo
one poignant, reassuring moment.

"I couldn't let them do this," he said quietly. "I'v
never been involved before. It's wrong. *Wrong.*"

"Vic, I'm scared."

He smiled faintly.

"No time for that. Let's go."

Victor's hand holding mine in comfort, we walke
noiselessly down the stairs, the sounds from the din
ing room at a peak. Dinner would go on as planned
But afterward, the Don would give the word. Th
girl upstairs must die. But the girl wouldn't be there.

Cautiously, glancing over his shoulder to make cer
tain we were unseen, Victor pulled the door oper
We moved out into the evening chill. I tugged m
coat closely about me, tensed my shoulders. Not fror
the cold. The door automatically locked itself behin
us. Never again would Andrea Grant walk throug
that door.

"I'll cut around to talk to the sentry," Victor whis
pered. "That'll give you time to get close to the ga
rage." His eyes scanned the sky. Overcast, murky. Th
kind of night for which the underground railroa
operators must have prayed.

"Victor, what about you?" My eyes clung to hi
"What will happen to you?"

"I won't be around—" His mouth silently framed the words. "I'll be on an Indian reservation, helping, I hope. Now beat it," he jibed, striving for humor. "Just make sure you stay in the shadows."

Victor cut up toward the dining room, its brilliant chandelier masked by the heavy draperies. I scurried across the south gardens, staying low against the lush shrubbery, swinging north toward the garage when I was a hundred feet away from the house.

I saw the array of drivers seated at a table in a brightly illuminated room above the garage. No shades, no drapes drawn against the night. Light spilling over the table, cluttered with cards and beer cans.

My eyes swung to the open garage. I saw Aldo, bent over one of the cars, feeding oil into its tank. I started as I inadvertently stepped on a twig that snapped beneath my feet. But Aldo was unperturbed. A night animal, he probably thought.

I waited, afraid to breathe, wishing Victor would hurry. But he was stalling, to make sure I had adequate time to take cover. I strained to listen, hearing every small sound in the night. There! There he was.

Victor moved into the spill of light from the garage, called out casually.

"Aldo? Aldo, come here for a minute—"

Aldo glanced up, startled at Victor's appearance here.

"Come on," Victor encouraged, gesturing broadly.

Aldo left the garage, crossed inquiringly to Victor. Victor dropped an arm about Aldo's shoulders, brought his head close to Aldo's. *Now.* I darted toward the garage, my breathing painful with apprehension as I ran, terrified that one of the men upstairs would come to a window, look out, realize what was happening.

I reached for the rear door of the Mercedes. Oh, let it open quietly! There—climb inside. Quickly! Close the door. No noise—please, no noise.

"Look, Aldo, it's rotten dull around here," Victor

was saying confidentially. "I can't drive with this on
How about shooting over to the ginmill with me
We'll have one drink, then come on back. Unless we
pick up some chicks," Victor said meaningfully.

"But I'm supposed to take care of the cars," Aldo
said doubtfully.

I dropped to the floor in the rear, tugged the
blanket down from the seat, spread it hurriedly above
me. The air in the car musty from being closed up fo
days. My heart thumped as I listened to Victor and
Aldo, coming into the garage, opening the front door
of the car.

"We'll go for a couple of quickies, forget the
chicks," Victor was soothing. "Nobody'll know you're
gone."

Aldo backed out of the garage, whistling in anticipation. Victor dropped an arm across the back of the
seat. A hand slid down toward where I lay, my face
uncovered so that I could breathe. Victor's fingers
pronged in the victory signal.

"Stuffy," Victor announced, and flipped the switch
that lowered the windows on his side of the car.
Gratefully, I gulped the rush of fresh air.

We rolled down the long, walled avenue, and I was
afraid that Aldo would hear my labored breathing
Victor was talking rapidly, loudly—a cover for me, I
realized. From Aldo's sly remarks, I gathered he believed Victor had already been hitting the bottle.

The car slowed down at the gates. Aldo whistled—
two longs, two shorts—for Rico. Aldo and Rico exchanged brief, ribald pleasantries, then the doors
swung wide. We were off the castle grounds!

Aldo gunned the Mercedes in a burst of high spirits, cannily sure Victor was in a rush to be at the
ginmill, having no inkling as to why. I lay still, tense,
in my uncomfortable crouch, the mountain air caressing my hot cheeks. We were rolling down the sharp
descent, where death would have overtaken me, except for Tony. Then the level stretch of road, and
another steep descent.

At last, Aldo was slowing down. The spill of red and blue light from the neon sign above the ginmill diffused about the rear of the car. I hastily retreated completely beneath the blanket. With Aldo retelling a ginmill joke, the two men emerged from the car. Their footsteps, heavy on the pebbled ground, fading away from me. A jukebox blaring raucously—briefly, violently loud as Victor and Aldo pulled the door wide to enter.

I heard the door close, thrust aside the blanket, pushed open the door, stumbled out of the car. Stared—momentarily galvanized—into the headlights of a car rushing toward me. A car that was pulling up to a shrieking halt ten feet away.

Terror riding herd over me, I ran. Toward the darkness behind the ginmill, into the protective custody of the woods. Running so fast I lost a shoe, but not daring to stop to recover it. Conscious of that figure chasing behind me in the blackness. Heavy, male footsteps, covering ground faster than I could ever manage.

An animal ran across my path. Involuntarily, I shrieked.

"Andrea—" Tony's voice, low, cautious. "Andrea, wait—"

"Tony! Oh, Tony—"

He was holding me tightly, murmuring soothingly to me, while I fought to regain my breath. He hadn't dared to call out my name before, lest Aldo hear me. Oh, Tony, Tony!

"Let's get back to the car," he whispered. "Cut out of here quickly. It's all right, baby—everything's all right."

In Tony's car we drove to the small house in the woods. Ted Hamilton was in the living room, with two men who were strangers to me. Ted introduced them, pushed me into a chair, brought me one of his inevitable mugs of coffee.

"Tony, how did you know to follow me?" My eyes clung avidly to his.

"We had a man stationed near the castle. He saw the Mercedes leave, radioed me. I followed to see what was up. We knew the meeting was on—we'd seen the limos ride up. I figured it might be you, cutting out. And then I saw you in the glare of the headlights—but you ran." He chuckled reminiscently. "I didn't want to scare you that way—but I didn't dare call out."

"Andrea, you saw them?" Ted probed sharply. "You saw the men?"

"I saw them." I nodded somberly.

As calmly as I could manage, I gave them a concise rundown of what had happened—including the full breakdown of what the syndicate planned.

"They're sure, with their power, their money, they'll be able to push through legislation to legalize marijuana. They want a good chunk of that scene when it becomes legitimate. At the same time, marijuana—a *starter drug*—creates more business for their hard stuff. Can you imagine the kids who'll wind up on heroin?" Ted swore under his breath.

"We have files here, Andrea," one of the men said gently—in the excitement I couldn't remember names. He moved toward me with a stack of photos. "Feel up to making identifications?"

"Hey, give her a break," Tony protested, an arm protectively about me.

"It's all right, Tony," I insisted quickly. I was away from the castle—beyond the cold hand of murder. "Bring on the photos."

I speedily pointed out the eight men who with Carlo and Nino formed the top echelon of the new syndicate. Ted assured me—even at this point—that this syndicate would never get off the ground. With the men identified, the FBI would concentrate on following them twenty-four hours a day, pick up the key men in the big families, under circumstances that would lead to indictment and convictions.

"What about the Congressman?" Tony asked gently. "Game to try to pick him out?"

"Show me photos," I shot back. To me, the Congressman was as rotten as the men gathered about the dining table at Castle Mazzini.

I identified the Congressman in a matter of minutes. I looked at him—and I remembered my father. I remembered the phone number of a syndicated columnist with whom he'd been close. For Dad, I was doing this.

"Can I leak this to a columnist?" I asked, and mentioned his name.

"Go ahead," Ted said, impressed with the potential of this. "Be our guest."

I put through the call, reaching not the columnist but his long-term secretary. Once, when Dad and the columnist had gone out for lunch together to talk shop, the secretary had taken me to Schrafft's for lunch. I told her the basic facts—that the Congressman was being wooed by the Mafia. I knew the next column would report this.

One of the men rustled up steaks for us, and we tried to relax from the unbearable tension of the evening. Later that night, Tony drove me all the way into Westchester County, stopping only once for coffee, to hide me out with his sister, who lived in the picturesque town of Armonk. Myrna was delightful—warm, intelligent, and affectionate. I gathered she realized she was welcoming a prospective sister-in-law.

The newspapers kept me up-to-date on what was happening. Carlo Mazzini's heart attack made page two in the tabloids. Within a week he was dead. Within two weeks, the FBI had brought in, and indicted, the eight men who had been present at the summit meeting. Surprisingly, Rico—with a promise of immunity—turned in Nino for attempted murder.

At the beginning it was Mama Mazzini, fearful of an occurrence such as actually happened, who persuaded Giuseppe to try to frighten me away—via the

two notes, the harmless snake in my bed. But it was
Nino who engineered—with help from Rico—the two
attempts on my life, and now Nino awaits trial. Carlo
Mazzini, as head of the syndicate, had ordered my
murder—which was expected of him—but Victor
could not allow this. I pray that Victor will find
peace—wherever he may be.

Tony and I will be married quietly early in September, when Suzy can be my maid of honor. This
morning, I drove into New York to shop for gowns. I
stopped in a candy shop along Fifth Avenue, and
ordered a box of fine chocolates shipped up to Mama
Mazzini, who lives on at Castle Mazzini. Only Mama
will understand.